Readers can't get enough of Kate Messner!

ALL THE ANSWERS

"An emotionally resonant portrait of a sweet girl whose struggles are firmly rooted in reality." —*Booklist*

"This story will appeal to Wendy Mass fans as well as those who love Messner's previous novels." —*School Library Journal*

"The lesson here—not only about the values of not knowing, but about managing oneself in the face of uncertainty— will resonate and, hopefully, inspire." —*BCCB*

Wake Up Missing

"Combines a fascinating concept with page-turning suspense." —Margaret Peterson Haddix, author of the Missing series and the Shadow Children series

"Loved it! Mystery, intrigue, danger, and creepy futuristic science set in today's world? Yes, please!" —Lisa McMann, *New York Times* bestselling author of *Wake* and *The Unwanteds*

EYE OF THE STORM

"A suspenseful science fiction story that keeps the reader engrossed from beginning to end." —*Library Media Connection*

"Plenty of action. . . . These heart-pounding scenes will be a hit." —*School Library Journal*

Sugar and Ice

The Brilliant Fall of Gianna Z.

ALL THE ANSWERS

ALL THE ANSWERS

Kate Messner

BLOOMSBURY

NEW YORK   LONDON   OXFORD   NEW DELHI   SYDNEY

For my editor, Mary Kate,
who asks all the right questions

First published in the United States of America in January 2015
by Bloomsbury Children's Books
Paperback edition published in April 2016
www.bloomsbury.com

Bloomsbury is a registered trademark of Bloomsbury Publishing Plc

For information about permission to reproduce selections from this book, write to
Permissions, Bloomsbury Children's Books, 1385 Broadway, New York, NY 10018
Bloomsbury books may be purchased for business or promotional use. For information on bulk
purchases please contact Macmillan Corporate and Premium Sales Department at
specialmarkets@macmillan.com

The Library of Congress has cataloged the hardcover edition as follows:
Messner, Kate.
All the answers / by Kate Messner.
pages   cm
Summary: Twelve-year-old Ava finds an old pencil in her family's junk drawer and discovers, during a math
test, that it will answer factual questions, so she and her best friend Sophie have a great time—and Ava
grows in self-confidence—until the pencil reveals a truth about her family that Ava would rather not know.
ISBN 978-1-61963-374-2 (hardcover) • ISBN 978-1-61963-375-9 (e-book)
[1. Supernatural—Fiction. 2. Questions and answers—Fiction. 3. Pencils—Fiction.
4. Family life—Fiction. 5. Self-confidence—Fiction. 6. Schools—Fiction.] I. Title.
PZ7.M5615All 2015   [Fic]—dc23   2014009072

ISBN 978-1-68119-020-4 (paperback)

Book design by Nicole Gastonguay
Typeset by Westchester Book Composition
Printed and bound in the U.S.A. by Berryville Graphics Inc., Berryville, Virginia
10 9

All papers used by Bloomsbury Publishing, Inc., are natural, recyclable products
made from wood grown in well-managed forests. The manufacturing processes
conform to the environmental regulations of the country of origin.

1

THE OPPOSITE OF MAGIC

The pencil didn't look magic.

It looked the opposite of magic.

It was the kind of pencil a parent might bring home from some boring financial-planning convention. The kind nobody wants, so it gets tossed in the kitchen junk drawer and hangs out with random nails and bits of string and rubber bands. That's where the pencil was until the morning of Ava Anderson's math test. She was totally out of regular yellow number-two pencils and had to go digging in the junk drawer looking for one.

The pencil was bright blue with yellow lettering that spelled out "EverQuest: Innovative Research Solutions." Ava didn't know what that meant, and she didn't care. All she cared about was having a pencil for math because if you showed up for Mr. Farkley's class unprepared, he gave you a look that could wilt a giant three-hundred-year-old oak tree right down to the ground.

And Ava was nothing like an oak tree. She was only twelve. She had skinny arms and spindly legs and wilted easily.

"Big test today?" Ava's dad hurried into the kitchen as she was dropping the pencil into her backpack. He opened the oven door, and black, blueberry-scented smoke billowed out.

"Math," Ava said, waving at the smoke. "Where are Gram and Mom?"

"Gram's not up yet—she wasn't feeling well last night—and Mom had an early meeting with some bigwig client who wants to invest in oil futures." Dad pulled an overflowing cake pan from the oven. "But don't worry, I've got breakfast covered." He juggled the hot pan to the counter and flipped it onto a plate. A charred something flopped out. "Ta-da! It's the world-famous Anderson's General Store giant blueberry muffin!" He looked down at the burned megamuffin. "It might be a tad overdone."

Ava poked through the charred crust with a spoon. It came out covered in batter. "The middle's not burned."

Dad sighed and took out the cereal as Marcus and Emma came downstairs.

Emma wore an orange dress with blue-and-white-striped tights and a name tag that read, HELLO MY NAME IS CLEEOPATRA.

"There's only one *e* in Cleopatra, Em," Ava told her.

"I spell it with two," Emma said, and poured herself a bowl of cornflakes. Emma had worn a different Magic-Markered name tag to school ever since she learned she was one of five Emmas in her second grade class, three of whom had last names starting with A. Instead of being Emma A-2, she'd decided to use a different name every day. Her teacher said that was fine as long as she wrote her real full name on papers.

"What's on fire?" Marcus asked, heaving his backpack onto the table. A coil of electrical wire rolled out and knocked over the cereal.

"Dad's world-famous muffin." Ava brushed the spilled cornflakes into her hand.

"I can't get them to bake evenly." Dad shook his head. "I thought for sure this was the one."

"You think they're all the one," Marcus said. "Like your world-famous sweet-pickle pie and your world-famous shrimp-and-Jell-O salad."

"I thought it would look cool. Like the shrimp were swimming." Dad's smile drooped.

"You'll come up with something, Dad," Ava said.

Ever since it was on the news that Shop-Mart would be opening a superstore in town, Dad had been obsessed with keeping the family general store alive. He figured if Anderson's could be world famous for something, people would come from all over and bring their wallets and everything would be fine. The trouble was, pretty much all the reasonable world-famous claims were taken by other stores in other towns. The dime store in Wakarusa, Indiana, had world-famous jumbo jelly beans. The Rainey Creek Country Store in Idaho had world-famous square ice cream cones. And Len Libby Candies in Scarborough, Maine, had claimed the world's only life-size chocolate moose and the world's largest chocolate animal sculpture in one fell swoop.

"I wish we'd thought of that chocolate moose first," Dad said, scraping the last of the muffin mush into the garbage.

There were moose in the mountains near Ava's town, so it would have been perfect. But you couldn't take somebody else's idea and make a slightly bigger moose.

"We could have a chocolate owl," Ava suggested. *Owl Moon* had been her favorite bedtime story when she was little. Mom had even taken her out to search for owls one night, just like the kid in the book. Ava never heard or saw one, but she still loved owls and tried to draw them. Mostly, they came out looking like confused penguins.

"Owls aren't big enough to be impressive," Dad said. "What about a chocolate bear? Or porcupine? Check online and see if that's taken."

"I'll look after school." Ava pulled on a sweatshirt, picked up her backpack and saxophone, and started for the porch to wait for Sophie.

"We could have a *Jell-O* moose!" Dad called after her. "Bet nobody's done that!"

The screen door slammed, and it was like a switch flipped in Ava's brain, sending jitters all through her body and twisting her stomach. Time to worry about the math test. It wasn't because she hadn't studied. Ava knew the formulas for finding areas of circles and triangles. She'd understood the lessons and had even helped Sophie with the homework.

But Ava knew she'd forget everything once first period started, like she always did when a teacher plunked an exam in front of her. She'd stare at the questions, her sweaty hand wrapped around her pencil. Her throat would get all dry. Then she'd have to cough, and Mr. Farkley was one of those teachers who scowled any time somebody coughed. Like it was on purpose, just to bug him. Teacher frowns felt like darts to Ava. She always ended up feeling strapped in her too-small chair, where she couldn't move and was doomed to sit quietly, blinking fast and chewing on her thumb, being darted to death while test answers slipped out of her head.

"Hey!" Sophie called, jogging up the driveway with her gymnastics bag bumping against her side. "How was your weekend?"

"Pretty good." Ava swallowed hard, but the worries were already stuck in her throat. "Are those new jeans?"

"Yep! I went shopping with Dad and Jenna at the outlets." She spun around. "Mom hates skinny jeans but she can't really do anything because Dad got them for me." Sophie skipped ahead on the sidewalk, through the red and yellow leaves. "Let's hurry so we have time to hang out with everybody."

"You can go ahead," Ava said, pulling a few index cards from her pocket. "I want to look over our math formulas."

"Didn't you study?"

"I always study," Ava said, "but as soon as I get near the math room, my heart gets thumpy and my face gets hot and I can't breathe and it's like I'm being smothered to death."

"Smothered in numbers?" Sophie raised her eyebrows. "I didn't know that could be fatal."

"It totally can," Ava said. "Death by linear equations."

Sophie laughed. "You'll be fine. Just remember pi R squared—you can picture a square-shaped rhubarb pie with a big R on it. Come on!" She grabbed Ava's hand and gave it a tug.

Ava could never say no to Sophie. Sophie was the only reason Ava survived preschool. She had taken Ava's hand and pulled her into the circle around the dress-up box to play. Ava never would have joined the group on her own. Back then, she'd been afraid of everything and everyone, not just math tests.

Okay, it wasn't just math tests. She was also afraid of the goats and thunderstorms and getting in trouble and airplanes and her grandma dying and her parents getting divorced like Sophie's. Also flesh-eating bacteria, ever since she'd seen that one episode of *Boston Med*.

"Let's run," Sophie said, taking off.

At least math was early in the day so she could get it over with, Ava thought, and she raced down the sidewalk, too.

THE VOICE IN AVA'S EAR

Breathe in four counts . . .
Then out four counts . . .
In . . . two . . . three . . . four . . .
Out . . . two . . . three . . . four . . .

Aunt Jayla, who was into yoga and meditation and other things
Ava's mom called "hippie hobbies" had told Ava that breathing
in through her nose and out through her mouth would help her
calm down, but it wasn't working today. All that nose breathing
only made Ava notice the smell of sharpened pencils, which
was like somebody screaming in her ear YOU HAVE A MATH
TEST TODAY! HAHAHA!!

"Is everyone *prepared* for class?" Mr. Farkley looked up and
down the rows, eyebrows ready to fly if he spotted some poor
pencil-less person. "Before we get started, I have forms for our

upcoming field trip. Bring them back signed with your ten dollars by next week." Mr. Farkley walked up and down the rows of desks, dealing out permission slips. Ava glanced at hers before she slid it into her backpack. "Adirondack Adventure Challenge" was printed at the top, in big dark letters. Below that was a photograph of a girl flying down some zip line thing with her mouth open, like she was screaming.

Ava supposed it was meant to look like fun. It didn't.

She stuffed the paper to the bottom of her backpack, down with the banana slime from when she forgot to take out her snack two weeks ago.

"All right. Desks cleared? Pencils out? Brains sharp?"

Mr. Farkley dropped a test on Ava's desk. She swallowed hard and picked up her pencil.

The first four problems were easy—tests did that to trick you into thinking everything would be okay—but the fifth one made Ava's throat dry and squeezy.

She should have reviewed those formulas on the way to school. What was Sophie's pie supposed to remind her of?

Ava pulled her scratch paper from under the test pages and doodled all the maybes.

Pi = π = 3.14

Pi R squared.

2 pi R squared.

Pi R.

2 pi R.

Pi R Something else...

The clock ticked.

Ava's eyes burned. She blinked a few times, then squeezed them shut. She knew she was going to have to multiply something by something, and she was pretty sure pi was involved.

Ava tried taking a few more four-count breaths.

She drew some pies on her scratch paper for inspiration. Apple . . . cherry . . .

They were not inspiring pies. They were lopsided and lumpy and offered no help whatsoever.

Ava doodled in big, bubbly letters.

What is the formula to find the circumference of a circle?

And a voice said, "Two pi R."

Ava jerked her head up. The kids around her were hunched over their papers working as if no one had said—or heard—anything. But whoever answered her question hadn't even bothered whispering. It was loud enough that the whole class should have heard.

"Ava?" Mr. Farkley was staring at her, eyebrows raised. "Is there a problem?"

"No. Sorry. I was . . . thinking." She looked down at her paper and carefully, slowly, circled the equation $2\pi r$. Whoever answered her question was right; she remembered now. So she did the problem, checked it over, and looked up again.

The voice couldn't have been Sophie's. She was way across the room. Luke Varnway was the only person sitting close to Ava, but the voice wasn't a boy's. It had sounded more like Ava's mom or Aunt Jayla. How come nobody else heard it?

Ava took a deep breath. Maybe it was like Aunt Jayla told her . . . if she could just calm herself down, the little voice in her head would give her the answer she'd studied. Maybe, after all the tests she'd bombed, her little voice had finally decided to show up!

It was about time. Ava took another breath and read the next question, about the area of the circle. Was that one pi R? Or pi R squared? Or two pi R squared?

Voice? Ava thought. *I could use some help here.*

She waited. But the voice in her head was already gone.

Come back! Ava thought. *Please?* She tried writing down the question, like she had before. Maybe she needed to see it on paper for her voice to kick in.

She wrote:

What is the formula for the area of a circle?

"Pi R squared," the voice said.

It was back! But it wasn't in Ava's head. It wasn't *her* voice at all. It sounded like it was coming from someone right there in the room. Ava looked around again. How could nobody have heard?

Ava made herself look down before Mr. Farkley saw her eyes wandering. She used the voice's formula to work out two problems.

But the next questions were about triangles, and Ava couldn't remember the triangle stuff.

So she wrote:

How do you figure out the third side of a triangle?

The voice said, "That depends on what kind of triangle it is. You'll need to be more specific."

Ava's mouth dropped open. She snuck a glance up at Luke, who was chewing his pencil, still working on the circle problems. He certainly wasn't the one talking to her.

Ava looked back at her paper. This triangle had a right angle; she knew that. So she wrote:

A right triangle

Ava waited. The clock ticked one of those big, echoey, you-are-so-running-out-of-test-time ticks.

But the only voice she heard was Mr. Farkley's. "Five minutes until the bell! I'll take papers up here when you're done."

A bunch of kids got up, walking past Ava's desk to drop off their tests.

Come on, Ava thought.

She tried again:

What is the formula for figuring out the third side of a right triangle when you know the first two sides?

If that wasn't specific enough, then the voice in her head was a big jerk.

But apparently, her voice liked the new question.

"A squared plus B squared equals C squared," it said. This time, Ava didn't bother looking up. She wrote down the formula and figured out the problem with a minute to spare, then tucked her scratch paper in her backpack and added her test to the pile on Mr. Farkley's desk.

"How'd you do?" he asked.

"Fine," she answered, like she always did. But this time, it was true.

3

SECRETS OF THE CHOCOLATE CHIP COOKIE CLUB

"How'd you do on the math test?" Sophie asked as they headed for their lockers before lunch.

"Pretty good, actually. The weirdest thing happened, though. It was like—"

"Ava!" Miss Romero called down the hallway, flapping a pile of sheet music so frantically it looked like she might be trying to get off the ground and fly. Miss Romero was tiny with a streak of green in her curly black hair. She looked like a hummingbird, darting and weaving through the maze of bodies and backpacks. When she reached Ava, she held up the music. "Sophie told me you're trying out for jazz band, so I pulled a few pieces I thought you might like. You'll need to play one of these and do a few bars of improvisation, okay?"

"Umm . . ." Ava looked at Sophie, who played drums and had told Ava last week that she should come to jazz tryouts. Ava was certain she hadn't said yes. She'd probably said something like, "That sounds interesting. I'll have to check it out," which in Ava-language meant, "That sounds terrifying, but you won't understand, so I'll nod for now and then forget to show up."

But here was Miss Romero. With music. "Tryouts are two weeks from today in the band room. You can come during study hall or after school, okay?" Miss Romero gave Ava the music and turned to go. "See you then!"

"We'll be there," Sophie called after her.

"*You'll* be there," Ava said as she and Sophie walked down the hall. "I never said I'd go for sure."

"Why not? What's the worst thing that could happen? You try out, it doesn't go well, and you don't get in. Right?"

"Wrong. I could show up with my saxophone and be so nervous that I pass out and hit my head on the floor, and then they'd have to call an ambulance, disrupting the auditions so no one else could try out either, and I'd be known for the rest of time as the girl who singlehandedly shut down the middle school jazz band. Also, my saxophone would be dented and Mom would kill me for dropping it, even if I managed to survive the fall."

Sophie laughed. "Fine. Ready for lunch?"

Ava hesitated. Her stomach was too tied up in knots for the chaos of the school cafeteria. Plus, Sophie's eighth-grade gymnastics friends had started sitting with them, and Ava couldn't tell if they liked her or not. "Actually, I need to go to the library." She didn't mention that her need had more to do with space and quiet than shelving books for the librarian, Mrs. Galvin.

"Okay . . . see you after school, then." Sophie turned toward the noise of the cafeteria, and Ava headed for the library. She stopped when she saw the sign by the door.

CHOCOLATE CHIP COOKIE CLUB TODAY

Mrs. Galvin held special activities in the library during lunch and after school. Chocolate Chip Cookie Club was a reading thing with poems and stuff. It used to be called Word Power, but not many people came to meetings until she changed the name.

Ava peered into the library. It was already busier than she liked. She understood that lots of kids liked the club, but she couldn't help feeling resentful about so many loud voices and crumbs invading what she'd come to think of as her sanctuary.

"Ava! I'm so happy you're here today. I think you'll love this group."

"I don't want to be in the club," Ava blurted and then felt bad when she saw Mrs. Galvin's smile fade. Ava liked Mrs. Galvin. She recommended good books and had cool quotes posted all over the library, but she and Ava just didn't think the same way.

The one time Ava had stayed in the library for a lunchtime writing workshop last year, Mrs. Galvin had waved her notebook around, telling everyone that "What if" was the greatest phrase in the English language. Ava couldn't have disagreed more. In fact, those were just about the *worst* two words in the universe. They led the charge for every one of Ava's worries. What if I fail math class? What if I lose my pencil before Mr. Farkley's quiz? What if somebody I love dies? What if there's a terrorist attack or an earthquake or a school shooting? What-ifs were not Ava's friend, and she had trouble trusting anyone who liked them as much as Mrs. Galvin did.

"I didn't know club was today. I was going to shelve books, but I don't have to." Ava started to turn away.

"That's okay. You can shelve during our meeting." Mrs. Galvin gave Ava a cart of books and hurried off to print copies of the club's poem for the day.

Ava started with the fiction. There were some some new quotes on the wall above the bookshelves.

A room without books is like a body without a soul. —*Cicero*
I have always imagined that Paradise will be a kind of library. —*Jorge Luis Borges*
The weak can never forgive. Forgiveness is the attribute of the strong. —*Mahatma Gandhi*
Any fool can know. The point is to understand. —*Einstein*

Ava smiled. Marcus would love the last one. He had an Einstein poster in his bedroom.

"Okay, let's get started," Mrs. Galvin told the kids at the tables. Ava could hear her voice from the other side of the shelves. "Sometimes, when you talk about poetry in English class, your teacher will want you to analyze every line and look for the similes and metaphors. Can anybody remember what those are?"

"A simile is a figure of speech that describes one thing by

comparing it to something else using the words 'like,' 'as,' or 'than,'" someone said. It sounded like Leo Kim, with a mouthful of cookie. "And a metaphor is a more direct comparison without 'like,' 'as,' or 'than.' Like if I said, 'These cookies *are* bites of heaven.'"

"Great," Mrs. Galvin said.

"Are we going to read a poem and pick out the similes and metaphors?" someone asked, and a bunch of people groaned.

"No," Mrs. Galvin said. "We're reading a poem that makes fun of them."

Ava was curious about that. It was hard to imagine a grown-up poet making fun of something serious like metaphors. She crept around the bookshelf and sat down at an empty table with a pile of books so she could listen while she pretended to sort them. Mrs. Galvin must have noticed; she wandered by and dropped a copy of the poem and a cookie onto Ava's table before she went back to the club.

The poem was called "Litany." Billy Collins, the guy who wrote it, started out like any other fancy poet by telling somebody—his wife or girlfriend, Ava guessed—that she was bread, a knife, a goblet, and wine. That already seemed like a lot of things for one person to be, but then he went on to compare her to pretty much everything else in the world. She was morning dew and a fish and an apron but *not* boots in a corner or a bunch of other stuff. And then the poet made a list of all the weird things *he* was—the moon and rain and some blind lady's teacup—and it was pretty clear he was totally mocking metaphors.

"That's awesome," one of the eighth grade girls said when Mrs. Galvin finished.

The boys thought so, too. They started making up their own metaphors.

"I am the touchdown in the final moments of the game," Luke Varnway said, holding his arms up to the ceiling.

Isaiah Gates scoffed. "Dude, you're the chewed gum underneath the bench."

"You're the smelly socks I left in my gym bag," shouted Alex Weinstein. "And the dog poop on the soccer field!"

That made Leo Kim laugh so hard he spit cookie crumbs all over the table, which made Mrs. Galvin raise her voice a little. "I think we have time for one more poem." She glanced at the library clock—"Maybe a short one"—and flipped through a fat book of poetry from her desk. "This is by Robert Frost," she said. "It's called 'The Secret Sits.'"

Mrs. Galvin read the poem in about five seconds flat. It was about a bunch of people dancing around in a circle trying to guess a secret, and the secret was in the middle, sitting there, doing nothing. That was the whole poem.

"I'll read it one more time," Mrs. Galvin said. Ava was glad. She'd liked the poking-fun-at-metaphors poem, but this one bugged her, and when Mrs. Galvin read it again, she figured out why. That secret was all kinds of smug about everybody trying to guess it and not knowing.

Mrs. Galvin looked up. "Anybody want to talk about this one?"

"Yeah," Alex said. "I think the secret's kind of a jerk."

Leo laughed, but Mrs. Galvin just nodded thoughtfully. "How so?"

Alex just shrugged.

"Because . . ." Ava surprised herself by answering out loud. Everyone turned her way, and her stomach tensed, but she kept talking. "We all try so hard to figure out what we're supposed to figure out and we get stuff wrong all the time and it's like . . . it's like the secret doesn't want to help us. Like it doesn't even *care* about all our questions."

Mrs. Galvin looked right at Ava. She blinked a few times, then nodded. "And when you're a person who really likes answers, that bothers you."

"Yes." Ava let out a rush of breath. "It does."

The bell rang then, and the room emptied out. Ava finished shelving her pile of books and started for the door.

"Ava?" Mrs. Galvin called from the table where she was pushing in chairs. "I'm glad you decided to join us."

"Yeah . . . I guess I sort of did."

"Will I see you for our next meeting?"

"I'll be here," Ava said. She was pretty sure she meant it.

4

THE PENCIL KNOWS

At the end of the day, Sophie was waiting at Ava's locker to walk home. "Hey, you put up a new Katina D. picture!" Sophie leaned in to check out the photograph and frowned. "Her hair's wet. Is this from the 'Wash the World Away' video?"

"I guess. I cut it out of one of Gram's magazines."

"Cool." Sophie started singing, "Let it rain . . . Let it pour 'cause I'm not gonna stand for your lies anymore," and did a few dance moves while Ava reached for her assignment book. "Wash the World Away" was their favorite Katina D. song. Ava loved the video of the band dancing in the pouring rain, even though Gram couldn't get past Katina's too-short skirt.

"Thanks for waiting." Ava slammed her locker and headed outside with Sophie.

"You never finished telling me about the math test earlier," Sophie said. "What happened?"

"It was like I kept hearing this voice...." Ava paused. She hadn't planned to bring up the test-voice again. It sounded so *weird*. In books and movies, it was always crazy people who heard voices in their heads. But this was Sophie, and Ava told Sophie everything. "The voice was ... telling me answers."

"I *knew* you were ready for that test." Sophie jumped up onto the curb, walked a few steps, and then stretched one leg way out behind her. The whole world was Sophie's balance beam.

"I don't know..." Ava waited for Sophie to start walking again. "The voice was weird. It felt *real*, like I could hear it out loud—not just in my head."

"I never heard anything." Sophie kicked an acorn along the sidewalk. "Maybe the math room is haunted."

"By a helpful ghost who knows formulas and only talks to me?" Ava shook her head. "You want to come over? Gram probably made cookies."

"Does Gram ever not make cookies?" Sophie had a good point. Gram was Ava's father's mom, and had lived with them since Ava was little. There were always cookies in the kitchen.

Sophie glanced up at her house. "Mom's home and I haven't seen her since Friday because it was Dad's weekend. Let me say hi and I'll come over in a while, okay?" She ran off, and Ava started up her own driveway. She hoped the goats wouldn't be out.

Dad had gotten Lucy and Ethel about a month ago. They were named after characters in his favorite old TV show, *I Love Lucy*. Lucy and Ethel were supposed to give milk, which Dad was supposed to sell in the store, which was supposed to draw business from miles around. But it hadn't worked out that way, so now they had a cooler full of weird milk that nobody bought and two grouchy goats who sounded like scary, screaming people when they bleated. When she wasn't hollering, Lucy was actually okay. She mostly ate grass and ignored everybody, but Ethel spent her whole life stalking Ava. She'd wait by the fence until Ava got home from school and then run at her.

Dad always laughed. "She won't hurt you." But Ava never stuck around to see what would happen if Ethel caught her. She'd veer off the driveway into the tall grass and end up covered in burrs and dandelion fluff.

Today the goats were fenced in, and that was good. Ava wanted to get to her room, close the door, and think.

"*Mehhh!*" Ethel bleated at her as she hurried toward the house.

"That you, sugarplum?" Gram called when the kitchen door slammed.

"Yep!" Ava grabbed two warm peanut butter cookies from the kitchen counter and headed for the living room. Gram was there, spraying water on a shirt on the ironing board and watching CNN. Gram's Jesus notebook was open next to the starch. She kept a list of all the situations in the world that she thought needed help so she could pray for them.

Ava knew that her name ended up on Gram's list a lot of days, too. Gram was the first person to notice when Ava was feeling especially anxious. She always caught Ava blinking too much, a sure sign Ava's insides were in knots. Then Gram would ask if she was okay, and Ava would insist she was fine, but she knew as soon as she left the room her name was going in that notebook right next to the prime ministers and presidents and war-torn nations in Africa.

Jesus had a mustache on the notebook cover now, thanks to Marcus and his black Sharpie. When Ava first saw that, she thought Gram would be furious, but Gram laughed and said if Jesus doesn't have a sense of humor, then nobody does.

"Got homework?" Gram said, turning over the shirt.

"Yep, I'm going to go start on it. Sophie's coming over later." Ava blew Gram a kiss and headed up to her room. If she had time after homework, she wanted to find a new quote for her wall. She'd started posting them on big pieces of paper, like Mrs. Galvin's in the library.

The bulletin board next to Ava's desk wasn't cluttered with party photos and ribbons and medals like Sophie's, but she did have a couple of ribbons from the fun runs she used to do in elementary school. Ava was pretty fast, even though the only running she did now was fleeing from Ethel. Besides the ribbons, the bulletin board held some yarn-and-feather crafts from her day camp last summer and a couple of school art projects—an Egyptian foil drawing and a black-and-white labyrinth design that had taken her forever.

She had two quote posters now, too, designed with colored

markers and her little owl cartoons. The first quote was from Henry Wadsworth Longfellow: *The best thing one can do when it's raining is to let it rain.*

Ava didn't know who Henry was, but she liked the quote because it reminded her of that Katina D. video. Ava wished she could be the kind of person who danced through a thunderstorm instead of hiding under the bed with dust bunnies and old stuffed animals. Sophie would do that, at least until Ava warned her that lightning kills an average of sixty people in the United States every year and made her come inside.

The other quote on Ava's wall was attributed to her mom's favorite writer, Maya Angelou:

I've learned that people will forget what you said, people will forget what you did, but people will never forget how you made them feel.

Ava liked that one because even though she messed up math tests and was afraid to try out for the track team and jazz band, she knew she was a pretty good friend. It was nice to think that mattered.

Ava thought she might add Mrs. Galvin's forgiveness quote from the library next, but she needed to do homework first, so she sat down at her desk and pulled out her math folder. The test review packet was right on top. Ava knew all the formulas now that the test was over. Maybe that voice in class really had been the voice in her head, finally doing its job.

Ava opened her desk drawer and took out a yellow legal pad. Mom ordered boxes of them to use for her financial stuff, and

Ava had come to like them, too. They made her feel organized and official and in control. This one had a dots-and-boxes game on the first page, from when Ava and her mom were waiting at the dentist's office a couple of weeks ago. Mom had promised Ava that if they kept busy finishing those boxes and writing their initials in them, Ava wouldn't have space in her brain to stress out about cavities and Novocain shots. Ava still worried, but at least the game had helped keep her mind off the drill sounds coming from the next room.

Ava turned to a new page on the legal pad, took a pen from the Popsicle stick container she'd made in third grade, and wrote:

What is the formula to find the circumference of a circle?

She listened.

Nothing.

Either Sophie was right and a ghost lived in the math room or it was one of those weird test-taking stress things. Whatever it was, having a magic answer-voice in your head was way better than being number-smothered to death.

Ava pulled out her science folder and took out the extra-credit paper Mrs. Ruppert had sent home. Ava was a big fan of extra credit. People who choked on every test needed all the help they could get. This time, Mrs. Ruppert was offering points to anyone who brought in goldenrod galls, these round things that formed on plants when goldenrod gall flies were feeding on them. Ava set the paper aside; she'd see if Sophie wanted to collect some with her later.

Then Ava found her worksheet on taxonomy and classification. Mrs. Ruppert required pencil, so she pulled the blue one from her backpack. The first few questions were easy enough that Ava didn't need her science book, but then she had to list the order of scientific classification and couldn't remember what came after "phylum."

Ava decided to try writing the question again, just in case repeating it made the little voice in her head show up.

Under her other question on the legal pad, Ava wrote:

What are the seven levels of scientific classification?

The voice answered, "Kingdom, phylum, class, order, family, genus, species."

Ava dropped her pencil.

It was back.

Ava looked around her room. This time, there was no chance the voice might be coming from someone else. Unless you counted Ruffles, the stuffed owl on her bed, she was alone in her room. Alone . . . except for some weird voice giving her answers to her science homework.

Ava still couldn't believe it was real, but she wrote down the seven levels of classification. The next question on the worksheet asked about some specific scientific names. Ava knew humans were *Homo sapiens* and dogs were *Canis domesticus*. But goldenrod gall flies were next, and Mrs. Ruppert hadn't mentioned them in class yet. Maybe the answer was in the book.

Ava started to pick up the book, but then her eyes fell on the questions on her legal pad. Maybe the voice would tell her. Could it possibly work, even with answers she'd never known? She wrote:

What is the scientific name for a goldenrod gall fly?

"*Eurosta solidaginis,*" the voice said.

Ava's mouth dropped open. She scribbled down the words, then looked up goldenrod gall fly in her science book index to check.

There it was, under a photograph on page 241: Goldenrod gall fly (*Eurosta solidaginis*).

Ava put the pencil down. She *knew* she'd never heard of that scientific name, so there was no way the voice was coming from her head. But why did it only work sometimes? Ava looked down at the math question scribbled on her legal pad. Maybe the voice was tired of math.

Ava ran her finger over the unanswered question, and the ink from the pen smudged a little. She looked at the science questions. Then she looked at the pencil. She picked it up and wrote:

What is the formula to find the circumference of a circle?

"Two pi R," the voice said.

Ava picked up the pen and wrote the exact same thing. The voice was quiet.

She wrote it once more with the pencil. There was the answer again, loud and clear. "Two pi R."

The voice wasn't coming from her head.

It was coming from the pencil. The blue pencil *knew* things.

"I'm here!"

Ava jumped, and the pencil went flying across her room.

"Nice welcome!" Sophie laughed and swooped down to pick it up. She handed it back to Ava. "What's up?"

"Sit down." Ava took a deep breath. "You're not going to believe what just happened."

5

M&M'S AND UNDERWEAR

"Are you sure you never heard that scientific name? *Totally* sure?"

"Sophie, I'm positive." Ava looked at the pencil on her desk. If she were Sophie, she'd be skeptical, too. She *was* skeptical, even though she was the one having conversations with a pencil.

"Ask it what I had for a snack after school," Sophie said.

Ava asked. The pencil answered, and she repeated its response. "M&M'S." Then Ava added, "But anybody who knows you would guess that." Sophie considered M&M'S to be a major food group.

"True." Sophie squinted at the pencil, then hid a hand behind her back. "Ask it how many fingers I'm holding up."

Ava wrote:

How many fingers is Sophie holding up?

"Four." The voice sounded bored.

"It said 'four.'"

"Try again." Sophie hid her hand three more times. Two fingers. One finger. No fingers. The pencil got it right every time.

Sophie's eyes were huge. "Do you know what this means?" She paced back and forth across the light green carpet in Ava's room. "You'll never have to study for another test!"

"Yeah, but . . ." A gnawing feeling grew in Ava's stomach. If the voice she'd heard during her math exam wasn't the little voice in her own mind, reminding her of what she already knew . . . if it was really this pencil talking and had nothing to do with what she had studied, then . . . "That's cheating, isn't it?"

"There's no rule about writing questions with your magic pencil. So why not?"

"It seems wrong." Ava already felt squirmy, knowing she hadn't really remembered those formulas for circles and triangles.

"Okay, fine. But there's so much stuff we can ask it." Sophie stopped pacing and looked at the pencil in Ava's hand. "Do you think it'll work for other people or just you?"

"No clue." Ava didn't see how the pencil could be answering questions in the first place. "But magic stuff usually has rules. At least in books."

Sophie put a finger to her pursed lips and looked at the ceiling. "It could be like a genie, and in that case, it'll probably only work for you. You're the one who found it."

"You think there's a genie in my pencil?" It hadn't occurred to Ava that somebody might be trapped in there. She put the pencil down.

"It's hard to say. Can I try writing a question with it?" Sophie asked.

"Okay." Ava moved aside so Sophie could write at the desk. "What are you going to write?"

"I don't know yet." Sophie's eyes darted around the room. "There are so many things I could ask it. I mean...oh!" She turned and started writing. Then she put the pencil down and looked up at the ceiling.

"It doesn't work for me," Sophie said after a few seconds. She looked disappointed.

"What'd you ask it?"

Sophie sighed and held up the legal pad so Ava could read it.

Who is the first boy I'm going to kiss?

"Will you try?" Sophie got up from the desk and motioned Ava to sit down.

"I don't want to know *that*!" Ava made a face. "I don't even want to *think* about that."

"Not *you*." Sophie sounded exasperated. "Me! Ask it who *I'm* going to kiss. Please?" She picked up the pencil and twirled it in Ava's direction.

"Oh! Okay." Ava took it, sat down, and wrote:

Who is the first boy that Sophie Chafik is going to kiss?

"What did it say?" Sophie was practically climbing onto the desk.

"Nothing."

"Huh. Do you think it only works if the question is about you?"

Ava looked at the pencil. "I don't think so. It told me how many fingers you were hiding."

"Well that stinks!" Sophie crossed her arms, then got a worried look on her face. "Ask it something else, okay? Make sure it's not broken."

"Like what?"

"Something easy. Like a math formula."

"Math formulas are *not* easy." But Ava wrote:

What is the formula for the circumference of a circle?

The voice said, "Two pi R," just as loud and clear as ever.

"It still works," Ava said.

"Well, why wouldn't it tell you who I'm going to kiss?" Sophie glared at the pencil. "Ask it why it won't answer my question."

"It probably won't answer that either." But Ava wrote:

Why wouldn't you answer the question about the first boy Sophie is going to kiss?

"Because *that* is not a *fact*," the voice said. It sounded cranky. "People have free will."

Ava carefully put the pencil down. She was a little worried that it was getting tired and maybe mad at them. And who knew what an angry pencil-genie might do?

"Did it answer?" Sophie moved Ruffles the Owl aside and flopped down on Ava's tie-dyed blue-and-green bedspread.

"Yeah. It said who you're going to kiss first isn't a fact, and that people have free will."

"Oh. That must be one of its rules." Sophie sat with her mouth scrunched up for a few seconds and then nodded. "I guess that makes sense. But it would have been cool if it told future stuff. We could have gotten lottery numbers for next week."

That felt like cheating to Ava, too, but she didn't say so.

"Hey!" Sophie bounced up from the bed. "That means it might still work for me. Can I try again?"

"Go ahead." Ava traded places with Sophie. Then she remembered the pencil's grumpy tone. "Be careful, though. I think it's getting tired of us."

"If it's a genie, it's not allowed to get tired of us." Sophie picked up the pencil, then gasped and put it down. "But wait . . . what if it *is* a genie and it'll only do a certain number of questions, like three wishes or something?"

Ava thought about that. "It's okay. You can try it." Even if there weren't many questions left, she'd want Sophie to have a turn. "What are you going to ask?"

Sophie frowned for a second, then laughed out loud and reached for the pencil. "I'm going to ask it what color underwear Mr. Farkley was wearing today!"

"Sophie, no! That is the grossest question ever!"

But Sophie was already scribbling. She finished and then doubled over in the chair laughing.

Ava really didn't want to know, but Sophie was laughing so hard she had to ask. "Okay, what? What did it say?"

Sophie held up a finger and tried to catch her breath. "Green . . . with . . . with . . . ." She started laughing again. "Yellow smiley faces!"

Ava laughed, too. She couldn't imagine how she was ever going to take a math test with a straight face again. How could someone so strict choose smiley face underwear?

"Ava, you girls okay in there?" a voice called from the hall.

"We're fine, Mom." Instinctively, Ava tugged open her desk drawer and brushed the pencil inside as her mom came in, balancing a cup of tea and a pile of folders, legal pads, and Money magazines in her arms.

"What's so funny?"

"Just the usual girl stuff," Sophie said, still giggling.

Mom glanced at the schoolbooks on Ava's desk. "How was your math test today?"

"Okay," Ava said.

"Better than okay," Sophie added. "Ava aced it."

"That's not really—" Ava began.

"That's great!" Mom leaned over, juggling her folders, and kissed the top of Ava's head. "You've had the force all along, my dear."

"It's power, Mom. Glinda said, 'You've had the power all along.' You're confusing The Wizard of Oz with Star Wars." Ava rolled her eyes. She and her mom had this thing where they quoted books they'd read together, trying to work the characters' sayings into real life, only Mom always messed up the quotes. Usually, Ava liked laughing with her about that. But lately, the whole silly tradition felt embarrassing when other people were around. Even Sophie. "We won't get the test back until later this week. But I think I did all right."

"Well, congratulations." Mom picked up the cookie napkins from Ava's desk and left, closing the door behind her.

Sophie let out a deep breath. "That was a close one with the pencil."

"Yeah . . ." Ava felt that way, too. But she hadn't really meant to hide the pencil from her mom. Had she? "Do you think we should tell somebody about this? What if it's dangerous?"

"Seriously? It's fine, Ava." Sophie pulled open the desk drawer, and Ava looked in. The pencil looked so ordinary, sitting there with the pens and paper clips. It was hard to imagine it doing anything bad. "Besides, nobody would believe us even if we did tell."

"Probably not," Ava said. What was it the professor in *The Lion, the Witch, and the Wardrobe* had told the kids when they got home from Narnia? Don't tell anybody about your weird magical trip unless you find out something similar happened to them? It was something like that, and it made sense. "I guess it's okay."

Sophie pulled the pencil from the drawer and twirled it between her fingers. "Let's go to the store and get a soda. And then we're going to have some serious fun with this thing."

6

JASON WHO?

When Ava and Sophie opened the door to Anderson's General Store, the bells on the handle jingled like always. Ava's dad looked up from the counter where he was writing something in Magic Marker. "Hey, girls! Grab a treat. How was your day?"

"Good." Ava tucked her legal pad under one arm and grabbed an atomic fireball from the candy counter. "Hey, Dad?" she asked casually, pulling the blue pencil from her pocket. "Any idea where this came from? It was in the kitchen junk drawer."

He shrugged. "Maybe from Grandpa's place. Mom and I swept about a year's supply of pens and pencils out from under his radiator when we were cleaning his apartment this summer. But finders keepers, I'd say. It's all yours." He went back to his lettering.

Sophie stretched a candy bracelet over her wrist and nibbled on one of the beads. "How is your grandpa?" she asked Ava.

Ava shrugged. "All right, I guess. But he seems even sadder

since he moved. He's had heart problems, so he can't live alone anymore, but I don't think he likes Cedar Bay." Grandpa, Ava's mother's dad, had been on his own since Grandma Marion died five years ago, but now he couldn't take care of himself and hardly ever talked. The doctors weren't sure if he was losing his memory or just depressed, but either way, they'd recommended Cedar Bay. Mom had called it a long-term memory care facility. All Ava knew was that it was full of old people who usually seemed like they were somewhere far away in their minds.

Ava's dad sighed. "It must be tough to give up living on your own." He put the top back on a Magic Marker and stepped back to look at his poster.

"Whatcha working on, Mr. Anderson?" Sophie asked.

"Something that'll have that superstore wishing it never made plans to open here." Dad held up the sign:

ANDERSON'S GENERAL STORE, HOME OF THE WORLD-FAMOUS MOUNTAIN MAN SANDWICH. He'd drawn a burly lumberjack next to the words.

"What's a Mountain Man Sandwich?" Sophie asked.

"I'm not sure yet."

"How does it get to be world famous?" Ava asked, sucking on her fireball.

"Well, hopefully if we *say* it's world famous, other people will catch on and say so, too," Dad said. "It's a proven strategy. There's a supermarket in San Francisco that advertises a world-famous turkey sandwich. It's a regular turkey sandwich, but they slapped 'world-famous' in front of it, and bingo!" Dad picked up a red Magic Marker and underlined "world-famous" on his sign. "Want to help brainstorm sandwich combinations?"

"Sure," Ava said.

"But not right now," Sophie jumped in. "We better do our homework first." She started for the door, and Ava understood. Sophie wanted pencil time.

It was warm for late October, so they went outside and sprawled under a maple tree that was still holding on to a few red leaves.

Ava poked around some weeds near the tree. "Think there are any goldenrod galls here? We get extra credit for science if we bring some in by Friday."

"How can you be thinking about some nasty bug larva when we have a magic pencil?" Sophie tapped Ava's legal pad. "What should we ask it?"

"I don't know." The whole thing was feeling weirder and weirder. Ava looked at the pencil as if it might grow teeth and bite her. "Soph, what if this pencil's cursed or something? What if . . . what if it wants to be paid for answering questions?"

"Paid how?"

"What if it wants our first-born children or our souls or something?"

Sophie laughed and made the pencil bounce through the air. "I'm the evil blue pencil," she said in a deep, growly voice, "and I want to suck out your soul . . ."

"I'm serious! That stuff happens in fairy tales all the time. And remember the story Mrs. Barnaby talked about in language arts last year? That Faust guy who wanted unlimited knowledge and traded his soul for it? What if this is like that?"

Sophie bit her lip, but she didn't laugh again. "Ava . . . take a good look." She held up the pencil. "It's not going to hurt you. It's just wood and lead and paint. But it can do something amazingly cool. Can you please stop worrying and enjoy it?"

Her words echoed in Ava's head. *Can you please stop worrying and enjoy it?* Ava had heard those words before. Spoken in Dad's voice, when she was afraid to try out for all-county band last year. In Gram's voice, when she'd splurged on a whale watch on a visit to Boston and Ava spent the whole trip in the cabin, tightening her life vest and blinking like crazy. In Mom's voice, when Ava was too nervous to stay overnight at Sophie's birthday sleepover just last month. Ava owed Sophie some fun.

"Okay." Ava took a deep breath and took the pencil. "What should we ask it first?"

"Ask it if any boys like you!" Sophie grinned.

Ava made a face. "What if it says yes? I'd never be able to look at them again." Ava knew plenty of girls in their class had crushes on boys and even boyfriends—if you counted holding hands on the way to lunch—but it seemed like those girls were on the other side of some strange invisible bridge. Sometimes, Ava thought Sophie was halfway across. "I'll ask it about boys who like *you* if you want."

"Okay!" It seemed like that was what Sophie wanted anyway, so Ava flipped to a new page on her legal pad and started writing:

Do any boys like

"Hold on!" Sophie leaned in, reading over her shoulder. "If you say 'like,' it might start listing boys who just sort of like me like a friend instead of boys who *like* me like me."

"So what should I ask?"

"How about . . ." Sophie looked up into the leaves just as one started fluttering down. She caught it, then turned back to Ava. "Let's try this. . . . What boys, if any, have romantic-type crushes on Sophie Chafik?"

Ava wrote that.

The voice gave a slightly disgusted sigh, then rattled off nine names. Ava tried to write them down, but the voice went too fast.

"What's it saying? What's it saying?" Sophie was bouncing.

"Hold on!" Ava held up her hand, then finished writing. "I didn't catch them all. I've got Robbie Henderson—you knew that, right?"

Sophie nodded. "Who else?"

"Craig Thomas, Jake Phillips, Howard Filion—"

"Eww!" Sophie recoiled. "He picks his nose in social studies."

Ava laughed. "Apparently, he's thinking of you the whole time."

Sophie fell over backward and kicked her legs in the air dramatically a few times, then popped back up. "Who else?"

"Shaun Gerstein . . ." Ava looked down at the page. "And Jason somebody? His name was too long, and I'd never heard of it."

Sophie's mouth fell open. "Jason *Marzigliano?* Ohmygosh, tell me it's Jason Marzigliano."

"Soph, you're drooling. I'm not sure."

"Ask the pencil to repeat it." Sophie gestured toward the notebook. "If it's Jason Marzigliano, I am going to flip. Literally."

So Ava wrote:

Could you please repeat the full name of the boy named Jason who has a crush on Sophie Chafik?

The voice sighed again, then enunciated every word. "Jason. Randolph. Mar-zig-li-a-no."

"Well?" Sophie was leaning so close Ava could smell the candy bracelet on her breath.

"It's him," Ava said, then couldn't help adding with a giggle, "and his middle name is Randolph. Jason *Randolph* Marzigliano. Who is he?"

But by then Sophie had flipped. Literally. She'd taken off running across the green and done a round-off back handspring. Then she plopped back down next to Ava. "Jason Marzigliano is that new kid who moved here from California. With the sort of shaggy brown hair? He does gymnastics, and he is unbelievably cute and I just cannot believe this!" She bit two more beads off her candy bracelet.

Ava laughed. She had to admit this pencil was kind of fun. "Let me try."

"Are you going to ask which boys like you?"

"No!" Ava tapped the pencil on her palm. She didn't want to know about boys, but she couldn't think of anything that seemed pencil worthy. "Maybe I'll ask it . . . what's for lunch in the school cafeteria next week."

"Ava, that's the boringest question ever! Go on the website if you want to know when meatloaf day is. Ask it . . . ask it what Katina D. is doing right this very second!"

"Oh, that's good!" Ava started writing. "It'll probably say she's in the recording studio."

"Or shopping for red cowboy boots! Or kissing her bass player in the rain!" Sophie squealed.

Ava finished the question and held up her hand for Sophie to be quiet.

"Right now," the pencil-voice said, "Katina D. is taking a nap."

Ava told Sophie, who let out a frustrated sigh. "Well, that's not going to make any headlines. Ask it what she did last night."

Ava asked and listened. "Oh! This is better. She went to dinner at some fancy French restaurant with Michael Jupiter. He's a singer, too, isn't he?"

"A singer?! He has the number one song on iTunes right now. And . . ." Sophie drummed the ground with both hands. "He's supposed to be going out with Tiffany Whittinger, the actress. This is awesome! It's a scandal!" Sophie got up and started pacing around the tree. "Ohmygosh, we should call one of those supermarket magazines with all the celebrity news and tell them. They'll do one of those splashy headlines with a photo on the front page, and we'll be famous!"

"Soph?" Ava held up the pencil. "We don't have a photo. Or anything else for proof. I don't think they'd be impressed if we said our magic pencil told us."

"Hmph." Sophie plopped back down on the grass. Her excited ideas got ahead of the rest of her brain sometimes. "Good point. But it's still fun for *us* to know. Ask it other stuff about her!"

So Ava asked the pencil what Katina D. had for dinner (escargot and steamed salmon with asparagus), who else knew about the date (no one, but that's going to change tomorrow because a waiter with a cell phone took their picture), and whether Michael Jupiter kissed her good night.

"Yes. Twice." The voice did not sound excited about this. But Sophie and Ava collapsed in helpless giggles.

"It's like we have a secret spy camera on the whole *world!*" Sophie said when she caught her breath. "This pencil is the best thing that has ever happened to anyone *ever.*"

"It really is." Ava flopped onto her back in the grass and looked up at the sun shining through the maple leaves. She had so many ideas for what to ask the pencil now. Where Katina D. bought the cool earrings she'd worn in the "Wash the World Away" video . . . what she liked to eat for dessert . . . what her favorite color was . . . what Michael Jupiter's favorite color was. What *anybody's* favorite *anything* was!

"You got all quiet." Sophie leaned up on her elbow to look at Ava. "You're not worried about the pencil wanting your first-born child again, are you?"

"Nope," Ava said, grinning. "I was just thinking about all the things we need to ask it tomorrow."

Sophie nodded. "We should make a list."

"Ava! Mom says dinner's ready at the house!" Marcus called from the store entrance.

Ava stood up and brushed off her jeans. "You make a list at home tonight, and I'll make one, too."

"Perfect!" Sophie hugged Ava and took off, cartwheeling over the lawn in the direction of her house.

Ava walked home and thought about what else she wanted to ask the pencil. She could ask anything about anybody—secrets about Hollywood stars, her favorite authors, her friends, her family. It was going to be a seriously long list.

7

LEMONADE, COOKIES, AND QUESTIONS

Ava meant to save the pencil to use with Sophie after school on Wednesday, but she didn't quite make it to the last bell. She pulled it out of her backpack twice during the day. The first time was right before lunch.

"You don't have to go to the library again, do you?" Sophie asked, balancing her lunch bag on her knee at her locker. "Come eat with us in the cafeteria. I miss you!"

Sophie's gymnastics friends, Maya and Lucy, were already waiting for her down the hallway. "Umm . . . let me check really fast, okay?" Ava told Sophie. She headed toward the library but then ducked into the girls' bathroom and took out the pencil. She didn't want to waste time finding paper, so she ripped a paper towel from the dispenser and wrote:

What do Sophie's gymnastics friends think about me?

Her hand was shaking as she finished the question mark.

"They don't know you very well, but they like you okay," the pencil said. "Maya thinks you're really nice but kind of quiet, and Lucy likes your sneakers with the bright green laces."

Ava looked down at her orange basketball shoes and smiled. Last summer, her cousin Shanika had visited from New York City and taught her how to lace them this fancy way that looked like a ladder. Lucy thought that was cool, and Maya thought Ava was nice. So Ava went to lunch instead of sneaking off to the library. It went pretty well.

The second time Ava pulled out the pencil was right after she finished running the mile in gym class. Mr. Avery asked her why she didn't try out for the cross-country team and if she planned to do track in the spring. Ava told him she didn't know, but when she got to the locker room, she took out the pencil and wrote:

Does Mr. Avery think I'd be good at running track?

"Yes." The pencil sounded like it wanted to add a sarcastic "obviously" to that answer, but it refrained. Ava wrote:

Who else is going to try out for the track team?

But there was no answer, and then she remembered the whole dumb free-will thing. She'd have to think more about track.

After school, Sophie came home with Ava. Sophie wanted to get right to the fun questions, but Ava said they had to do homework first or they'd never get to it. So they did their English vocabulary page and then asked the pencil where they could find goldenrod galls. It told them, and they snipped a bunch from stalks in the field behind the store. Then Sophie ate pizza with the Andersons. She and Ava were headed upstairs with the pencil when Ava's dad said, "Everybody ready for family night?"

Wednesday was family night at Cedar Bay Nursing Home. Every Wednesday after dinner, attendants wheeled the residents down the long yellow hallway to meet with family members. Everybody sat in folding chairs, drank warmish, watered-down lemonade, and ate cookies while they waited for the seven o'clock show, usually some local church choir or little kids' ballet class or high school string ensemble.

Nobody talked much on family night. A few of the residents couldn't speak because they'd had strokes. Some, like Ava's grandpa, could talk but were too sad or grumpy to say much. Others had dementia and didn't know what was going on around them. When the dementia people did talk, it didn't always make sense.

Mr. Clemson, who was a firefighter a long time ago, worried about imaginary burning buildings. "Get down!" he'd hollered at Ava when she walked by during family night once. "Stay low and head for the exit!"

Mrs. Grabowski, who had a stroke two years ago and couldn't talk at all, always wore a pale purple pantsuit and tapped her feet to the music. Her white sneakers were too clean ever to have seen grass.

Mr. Ames spent family night slapping his knee enthusiastically, though never quite in time to the music. Mrs. Raymond, who wore pastel sweatshirts with cuddly animals embroidered on the front, tipped her head back and forth to whatever song was playing. And Mrs. Yu sat perfectly still except for her mouth. She always looked like she was chewing, even though she never ate the cookies.

The Snoozy Gang—that's what Ava and Sophie called the residents of the back row who nodded off as soon as the concert started—always woke up with a start at the end.

Then there was Grandpa, who scowled under his pulled-down baseball hat and complained about the music, if he said anything at all.

Mom never missed family night, but she never had much to say to Grandpa. They hadn't gotten along since Grandma Marion died. Ava's mom didn't talk about why, but her dad told her once it had to do with Grandpa's lifestyle and choices. Ava didn't ask about it after that. She just went with Mom and everyone else to the nursing home on Wednesdays and ate the cookies.

Family night wasn't negotiable, so Ava and Sophie put their pencil plans on hold and piled into the Andersons' minivan for the drive to Cedar Bay.

"You brought it, right?" Sophie whispered to Ava once they got settled in the community room and the others had gone to check out the snack table.

"Yep." Ava slipped the pencil and her legal pad out of her backpack.

"I've got my list, but I was thinking," Sophie whispered. "We should find out if it can answer bigger questions."

Ava frowned. "Bigger how?"

"Like important world things. Like..." Sophie grabbed a newspaper from one of the folding chairs and scanned the front page. "Ask about the election—not who's going to win, but maybe... you know how the candidates are always looking for rotten things to say about one another? Ask it if Senator Tobinovitch has ever broken the law."

"Ha! My dad would love that question. He can't stand that guy." She wrote:

Has Senator Rodney Tobinovitch (the one running for president) ever broken the law?

Immediately, the voice in her ear said yes.

"It says yes."

"Ohmygosh!" Sophie's eyes lit up. "Ask what he did and when and everything!"

So Ava wrote:

When, where, and how did Senator Rodney Tobinovitch (the one running for president) break the law?

"He sometimes drives in excess of the speed limit," the voice said. Ava waited. But the pencil didn't say anything else.

She looked at Sophie. "He drives too fast."

"That's it? Everybody drives too fast."

Ava shrugged and looked up just in time to see her family coming back to the chairs. Emma was scowling down at her cookies.

"Cookies look good, Em," Sophie said, smiling.

"They're *tiny*, but I only got to take two," she grumped. "And call me by my real name." She pointed to her HELLO MY NAME IS RAPUNZEL tag.

"Settle down, Rapunzel," Dad said, ruffling her hair. "Grandpa's coming."

When the attendant wheeled Grandpa into the community room, Dad said, "Good to see you, Hank. You're looking terrific."

Grandpa grunted.

Then half a dozen Irish dancers showed up, wearing long-sleeved white shirts and plaid skirts and vests. They were sweating like crazy even before they started hopping and kicking.

The music was so fast Mrs. Raymond could hardly keep up with her head tipping. Mrs. Grabowski's tapping feet looked as if they might carry her right out the door and down the street. But Grandpa never looked up from his hands.

"They're terrific, aren't they, Hank?" Dad said when they finished and everyone was clapping. He leaned over to Grandpa. "Did you like the music?"

"No."

"No?" Dad smiled and hummed part of the song, doing a little chair dance. "I thought it was pretty lively."

"Tinny, whiny garbage. That's not music." Grandpa kept looking down at his fingers, all wrapped together, as if he might find the real music there.

Sophie got a sparkle in her eye and pulled her iPod out of her purse. "Want to hear something better?"

"Tell me you're not about to torture Grandpa with Katina D." Marcus smirked.

"Why not?"

"Soph, I don't think that's a great idea," Ava said, but Sophie was already poking her ear buds into Grandpa's hairy ears.

Grandpa swiped them away. "Garbage!" he grouched, and started babbling about some old nightclub in Manhattan where they played *real* music and knew how to make a decent whiskey sour, too. Then the nurse came and said it was time to go back to his room.

Sophie looked at Ava. "I'll put different music on there for next time. Maybe we can find something he likes."

"We'll see you next week, Hank," Mom said. She never called Grandpa "Dad." In the past, Ava had always chalked that up to the way things were, but she found herself wondering about why they didn't get along.

Now, she had a way to find out.

8

JUST LIKE PETER PAN

"I'm not sure this was faster than looking it up in the book," Ava said, as Sophie scribbled down the question for number ten on their worksheet after school the next day.

"Shh!" Sophie held up her finger, tipped her head, listened, and wrote down the answer. "I know. But this was more fun." She tucked her finished worksheet inside her folder and twirled the pencil in her fingers.

"Ava!" Marcus shouted from down the hall. "Mom says you gotta set the table."

"It's your turn," Ava called. "I did it last night."

Marcus appeared in the doorway. "I have a physics test tomorrow and Mom says that takes priority. Which makes tonight your night, too." He stuck out his tongue and ducked just in time to avoid being hit by the pillow Ava threw from her chair.

"Why can't he study after dinner?" Sophie asked.

Ava sighed. "He decided his ninety-seven-point-three grade point average isn't good enough, and Mom's totally backing him up." Marcus had always been a good student, but lately all he ever did was study, as if every point on a test was a matter of life or death.

Ava tucked the pencil in her backpack—the last thing she needed was for Marcus to come by and swipe it—and she and Sophie headed down to the kitchen. Gram was pulling mac and cheese from the oven. Dad was slicing a loaf of Italian bread from the store, and Marcus was on the computer. He took time out from his crucially important homework to smirk at Ava when she opened the cupboard to get plates. Ava's mom was ripping up lettuce for salad and listening to the presidential candidates on the radio.

"I can't believe Governor Tedds expects hardworking people to buy that load of—"

"Alisha . . . ," Dad said, raising his eyebrows and glancing at the girls.

"Mom's having a terrible, horrible, no good, very bad day," Ava said. "Like Alexander in the story." She thought their book-quoting game would make her mom smile.

It didn't. She pursed her lips together and tore the lettuce a little more violently.

"Glad I'm not part of that salad," Dad said, laughing. He leaned in to kiss Mom on the cheek, but she dodged him.

"Just because your candidate has an edge in the Northeast," she said, shaking her head.

"When you guys get divorced," Marcus said, "I'm blaming the two-party political system."

"Sophie's parents are divorced and now she gets to have two houses," Emma said, dragging her stuffed boa constrictor to the table.

"It's not as cool as you'd think," Sophie said. "You have to search twice as many places when you lose a library book."

Emma looked up at Mom. "Are we getting divorced?"

"No, we are not," Mom kissed the top of Emma's head. "You're stuck in this one house, Miss Emma."

"I'm Jupiter today," she said, pointing to her name tag.

"Is she going through all the planets?" Sophie whispered to Ava. She looked alarmed. "Whatever you do, make sure she doesn't go to school with a name tag that says 'Uranus.'"

"Sit down and eat before this gets cold, Jupiter," Gram said, sprinkling more parmesan over the mac and cheese.

Ava's parents had a rule, no politics at the dinner table. So the talk turned to physics homework and Dad's latest idea—world-famous giant cheese puffs.

"I think they could be a hit," he said.

"Ava, you're not eating much." Mom raised her eyebrows at Dad. "Were they eating junk food at the store after school again?"

"No," Ava said. "I'm just not hungry." The truth was, her parents' arguing had given Ava a stomachache. No matter how many times her mom said they were just having "thoughtful dis-course" as she called it, Ava couldn't help worrying that things might get worse. And she didn't want two houses. Ever.

So Ava kept poking her macaroni around her plate and looked around the table. Gram was doing the same thing, Ava noticed. Maybe she was worried about something, too.

After dinner, Ava and Sophie hurried upstairs. Sophie rummaged through Ava's bag looking for the pencil and pulled out the Adventure Challenge permission slip. "Hey! We were supposed to turn these in." She sniffed it. "This smells like banana."

"You can put it back. I'm not going."

"Ava, you *have* to go! It's the coolest field trip ever!"

Ava flopped onto her bed, and Ruffles the Owl bounced off onto the floor. "If you like plummeting to your death in the woods."

"It's totally safe, Ava." Sophie swooped down, picked up Ruf-fles, and perched him on Ava's pillow. Then she plopped down next to Ava. "My mom read about it on the website before she'd sign mine. You wear a harness, and you're always connected to a safety cable, so there's absolutely no way you can fall and die."

"Well, that's good." But Ava knew there was always a way. What if the harness came unclipped? What if the safety cable broke like the rope Dad had used to tie Ethel to the fence that day she got loose and they found her down the street eating the

Morgans' mail? You could totally fall and die then. Any field trip with the word "adventure" in the title had entirely too many what-ifs swirling around it. "I'll think about it," Ava said. That was usually enough to shut Sophie up.

But not this time. "Come on, Ava. We're even going to practice in gym class. Mr. Avery told us he has some minicourse he's going to set up with low balance beams and stuff. It's going to be *so* fun. Have you seen the videos online?"

Ava shook her head.

Sophie jumped up. "Come check out the website with me, and if it doesn't look awesome, I promise I'll leave you alone, okay?"

She led Ava downstairs to the computer, found the website, and clicked to start a video. "Tell me this doesn't look like fun."

On the screen, a teenage girl with her hair in pigtails was holding on to ropes, walking across a bridge made of wooden rods that wobbled and swung all over the place. Just watching her was enough to make Ava's knees feel like jelly.

Then there was a kid climbing on a rock wall, putting his feet on tiny ledges that didn't look nearly big enough for feet. Ava watched the video people tightwalk from tree to tree, way above the forest floor. They crossed rickety bridges over rocky streams, clipped themselves onto zip lines, and went flying through the trees. "I feel like Peter Pan!" the pigtail girl squealed.

There was no way Ava would feel like Peter Pan up there. She would feel like a big baby. She reached over and stopped the video.

"So will you go?" Sophie bounced up and down a little.

"Maybe."

"Just go. If you don't like it, I'm sure you can sit and read or something." Sophie's cell phone chimed with a text, and she looked down. "Shoot. Mom wants me home. But promise me you'll come, okay? Just *try*."

Ava sighed. "What if" may have been her least favorite phrase in the English language, but "just try" was a close second. When Ava had just tried to go on the boat ride in third grade (What if it sank? What if the lake was rough?), she'd spent the first hour of the trip throwing up over the railing. When she'd just tried to spend the night at Sophie's sleepover (What if she got sick? What if something happened to her parents while she was gone?), she'd stayed awake all night until Mrs. Chafik found her crying in the kitchen and called her mom to come get her.

There would be no just trying on the Adventure Course of Doom, Ava decided. But there was only one way to get Sophie to stop asking and go home.

"Fine. I'll try." Ava's twinge of guilt at the lie grew into a giant stomach pit of shame after Sophie hugged her before she ran out the door.

Ava waved. She promised herself she'd make it up to Sophie with extra pencil time tomorrow.

9

STUPID FREE WILL

After Sophie left, Ava went to her room and did her math homework without any pencil help. She made a new poster with Mrs. Galvin's forgiveness quote on it and doodled what she hoped were some forgiving-looking owls in the white spaces. One turned out pretty good, but the other two resembled penguins again. And their expressions looked more surprised than forgiving.

Ava put the new poster up on her bulletin board next to the other quotes and the dream catcher she had made at craft camp in fourth grade. Then she popped a saxophone reed in her mouth, found her jazz tryout music, and discovered an orange sticky note on top, with a note from Miss Romero.

Didn't have this in my library,
but I borrowed it from a friend for you.
Remembered how much you love Titanic!

There were stars on the sticky note, like this was the song Miss Romero really wanted Ava to play. The thing is, they'd only talked about the *Titanic* once, when Ava was reading a newspaper article about a *Titanic* artifact exhibition before her music lesson. Miss Romero had said, "Oh, do you like *Titanic*?" And Ava had answered yes. She'd meant the ship and the story of the iceberg, not that sad movie they made, but Miss Romero started going on and on about Leonardo DiCaprio then, and Ava couldn't get a word in edgewise.

So now she had this music for "My Heart Will Go On." Ava put her sax together and tried playing it. She was pretty good at sight-reading, and this song wasn't hard, but the whole time she was playing it she kept picturing all those actors and actresses floating around in the sea with their shivery blue lips. Ava tried to clear her mind and feel the music, but once her brain got going on something she couldn't turn it off.

Ava stopped halfway through the song and flipped through the rest of the music. Nothing else had stars, but maybe there was something Miss Romero would like as much as the frozen bodies song.

Ava leaned over, pulled the pencil and legal pad from her backpack, and scribbled:

Which jazz tryout song does Miss Romero like best?

"Thelonious Monk's 'Straight, No Chaser,'" the voice answered.

Ava found that one, but there was too much black on the page, too many quick notes. She played the first few lines.

Ba-da-ba-do-BA, ba-da-ba-da-ba-do-BA, ba-da-ba-do-BA, ba-da-ba-do-BA-WAH...

Knowing Miss Romero, Ava understood why she'd like this song. To Ava, it felt too frantic and panicky.

Ava put her saxophone down and sighed. Maybe she'd stay home the day of those tryouts. She checked the date Miss Romero had scribbled on that Post-It note—November 12. That was the day of the field trip, too. Ava's heart lightened a little. It was a bonus if you could avoid two awful things with one sick day.

It wasn't that Ava didn't want to be in jazz band. She loved the feeling of playing with a group because everyone sounded big and rich and brave, playing together. But aside from the what-to-play problem, there were older kids in jazz band. What if she wasn't good enough to play with high school musicians? What if she showed up to try out and they laughed? What if she threw up on her saxophone before she even had a chance to audition?

Ava tried the Thelonious Monk song once more, but she had already what-iffed herself out of enjoying the practice time even a little. It was getting late anyway, so she started taking her saxophone apart.

"Ava?" Mom appeared in the door with a laundry basket in her arms. "Get ready for bed, all right? I'll be back to read."

"Okay." Ava put her music away, brushed her teeth, and got into her pajamas. "Ready!" she called after she climbed into bed. Mom came back, laundry free, and flopped into bed next to her with their book.

When Ava had learned to read chapter books herself in second grade, she'd told her mom she didn't need a bedtime read aloud anymore. Mom said that was too bad because she still needed it, so Ava should move over and make room. Five years later, Mom hadn't changed her mind, and Ava was secretly glad. It was the only time she really had Mom to herself, with no phone pressed to her ear.

"Were you reading ahead?" Her mom frowned at the bookmark.

"Maybe a little." Ava reached over and flipped back a few pages in *The One and Only Ivan*, about a gorilla who lives in this crummy shopping mall exhibit with an elephant. "We were here, where the new elephant comes."

Ava snuggled into her pillow and listened. She liked Ivan. He worried a lot, too. Being a gorilla in a shopping mall was a lot like being a kid. So much was out of your hands, and if you were a worrying kind of person, that just made you worry more.

Mom finished the chapter, closed the book, and looked at Ava. "You okay tonight?"

"I'm all right." She paused. "I don't like it when you and Dad argue about election stuff."

"We weren't arguing. We were *debating*." Her mom laughed a little. "Honey, we've been canceling out each other's votes every November for eighteen years. I promise it's nothing to worry about."

"I know." That wasn't true, though. It *was* something to worry about, and Ava did. She kept thinking about what would happen if her parents got divorced. "It's hard to stop worrying once you start."

"I know. I guess today was kind of a terrible, horrible, no good, very bad day." Mom smiled a little. "But some days are like that."

"Even in Australia," Ava added, true to the book they'd read together when she was little.

"Night." Mom kissed Ava's forehead and stood up. "Have a good sleep." She turned out the light and left.

Ava got up and turned the light back on. Because she had the pencil now. She didn't have to wonder if her mom was telling the truth. She could check. She flipped to a new page on the yellow legal pad and wrote:

Are my parents going to get divorced?

The pencil didn't answer. Ava's throat got tight. What if they were and the pencil didn't want to tell her? She tried again:

Will you please tell me if my parents are going to get divorced?

"No," the voice said, and Ava felt relief wash over her. But then she realized she wasn't sure what question it was answering.

Did you mean no, my parents are not getting divorced, or no, you won't tell me?

"No, I can't tell you."

Why not? Ava wrote.

"Because your parents have free will like everyone else," the voice said crisply.

Stupid free will again. Didn't the pencil understand she

needed to know so she could get some sleep? How could she make it answer? Ava bit the top of the pencil, thinking, then quickly took it out of her mouth. It was probably a bad idea to bite something that talked. The pencil already seemed impatient with her; nibbling on it wasn't likely to improve their relationship.

Finally, Ava had an idea. Sophie's parents had gone through a whole lot of lawyer stuff before they got divorced. It took months before anything really got done. So Ava wrote:

Have my parents been to see a lawyer to talk about getting divorced?

"No," the voice said.

There. There was her answer.

Ava put the pencil down, got in bed, and pulled the covers up to her chin. She could cross one worry off her list.

For now.

10

SCIENCE CLASS PSYCHIC

When Ava came down for breakfast Friday morning, Dad was scribbling on a big piece of paper. "Give me more," he urged Marcus and Emma. "If we keep brainstorming, something amazing is going to come up."

"Are you giving up on the world-famous Mountain Man Sandwich?" Ava asked.

"Nobody seemed excited about it," Dad said. "I don't understand. There's a place in Rochester that has a world-famous garbage plate—that's what they call it, for real. It's nothing but a burger and home fries and macaroni salad covered with hot sauce, and they do great. How is a *garbage* plate better than a Mountain Man Sandwich?" Dad shook his head. "Anyway, let's move on. Who has a new idea?"

"World's Biggest Pineapple!" Emma shouted, dribbling orange juice down her HELLO MY NAME IS POLYESTER name tag. Dad wrote that down.

"Pineapples don't grow here," Marcus said. He poked at his phone for a few seconds. "Plus there's already a World's Biggest Pineapple in Australia."

"I want to go there!" Emma wiped the juice off her name tag. "They have koala bears."

"Most fruits and vegetables are spoken for," Marcus said. "Castroville, California, has the world's largest artichoke. Ellerbe, North Carolina, and Strawberry Point, Iowa, both claim they have the largest strawberry. I guess the North Carolina one is a building painted red with black seeds, and the Iowa people say that doesn't count, so their statue is the biggest. And Gaffney, South Carolina, has the world's largest peach at the top of a water tower." He squinted at his phone. "It looks like somebody's butt."

"Peach butt! Peach butt!" Emma sang, then collapsed in a fit of laughter.

"Come on, you guys . . . focus," Dad said. "Any ideas, Ava?"

"World's biggest . . . I don't know." Maybe she could ask the pencil later which "world's biggest" and "world-famous" things were available. Though that seemed like the kind of question the pencil might have issues with. The pencil had a lot of issues.

"Let the kids get ready for school," Gram said, clearing dishes. "Busy day for you guys?"

"We're playing recorders in music class," Emma said.

"That'll be fun," Gram said.

"World's biggest sap bucket!" Dad exclaimed, writing furiously. "I bet nobody's got that."

"We can look it up later," Ava said, then turned to Gram. "I have a vocab quiz in English."

"And I've got a physics test," Marcus added.

"Well, good luck," Gram said. "I'll say a prayer for you both."

"I don't need a prayer, Gram." Marcus stood up and slung his backpack over his shoulder. "I'm prepared."

"I'm sure you are." Gram blew him a kiss. "So you go answer questions. I'll be here praying, and between the two of us, we'll have it covered."

Ava laughed. She didn't know any other families that were so weird about religion. Her parents believed in God but didn't go to church or talk about it much. Her aunt Jayla in Vermont was a Buddhist or something. Gram was Gram. And Marcus had proclaimed himself an atheist last year. Ava loved going to church with Gram because the stained-glass quiet felt so calm, but she still wasn't sure what she really believed. Maybe she'd ask the pencil which religion was actually right.

Ava loaded her backpack with her books and folders and the bag of goldenrod galls. She slipped the pencil into the smallest pocket, put on a jacket, and headed out to meet Sophie.

"*Mehhh!*" Ethel screamed as Ava ran past. She splashed into a puddle and sighed. Quiz days were bad enough without having a soggy sneaker.

Sophie was waiting at the bottom of the driveway, twirling around with her purple umbrella. "I have the best idea ever."

"What's that?" Ava was pretty sure it was about the pencil. The pencil seemed to have taken over most of Sophie's brain.

"We can open up our own business, like we're psychics, and we'll answer questions and tell the future and—"

"But we're not psychics." Ava pulled her hood over her head. It was starting to rain. "And the pencil doesn't tell the future anyway."

Sophie jumped up onto the curb and walked on her tiptoes. "We won't have to tell the future; we'll just *know* things, like who likes who and where lost homework assignments are and stuff. It'll be fun!"

"Maybe." Ava had actually planned to leave the pencil in her locker today, so she wouldn't be tempted to use it on the vocabulary quiz. But by the time they got to school, the first period bell was ringing, so she didn't have a chance.

Ava still had the pencil in her backpack when she got to English. That's where it stayed during the quiz. She only longed for it once, when she couldn't quite remember what the word "obdurate" meant, but she guessed. Even if she got it wrong, she'd have a grade of ninety.

"You have the goldenrod gall things, right?" Sophie asked on the way to science.

Ava nodded. "We're doing a lab with them today."

When they got to Mrs. Ruppert's room, every table was set up with paper towels and a steak knife, as if they were going to eat the goldenrod galls for a snack.

"Have a seat so we can start," Mrs. Ruppert said from her demonstration table. "We're going to be cutting open the goldenrod galls you brought today. If you don't have any, that's okay;

I have extras. You'll insert the knife partway into the gall and then twist it." She did that, and the gall split open. "What we're looking for is . . ." Mrs. Ruppert squinted at the two halves. "Oh, this is gorgeous!" She sounded as if she'd found gold or at least chocolate inside, but when she walked around, all Ava saw was a wiggly, white grub type thing.

"Here we have a goldenrod gall fly larva," Mrs. Ruppert went on. "This one's lively, but when you cut open your galls, you'll find that not all the larvae will have fared so well. Some will have fallen prey to parasitic wasps or beetles. And if there's a visible hole in the gall, your larva may have been eaten by a downy woodpecker or chickadee. Ready to get started?"

Ava and Sophie were in different groups for science. Sophie went off to a table with Alex Weinstein and Leo Kim, while Ava left her backpack by the door and set to work cutting open galls with Luke Varnway and one of the Mason twins—Kylie or Marissa. Ava could never tell the difference and figured it was rude to ask.

It was a pretty neat lab. Ava's group got off to a rough start when Luke forgot they were supposed to insert the knife halfway and twist, so he sliced their first larva right in half. But then they found a whole bunch of live larvae and two galls where those special wasps had broken in and eaten the larvae.

"Whoa! Do that again!" someone called from a table across the room. Ava wondered what they'd found. When she looked up, she saw two lab groups gathered around Sophie. But Sophie

wasn't holding a goldenrod gall with a larva or wasp or beetle.
She was holding the pencil.

Ava put down her knife and rushed over. "Why'd you take
that out of my backpack? What are you doing?" she whispered.

"I'm showing everybody how we've been working on our
psychic powers." Sophie grinned, then started writing on a note
card in her hand.

"Oh, great goldenrod gall fly spirits . . ." Psychic Sophie
whispered as she wrote. "Tell me what rests in the great
unknown of the goldenrod gall in Alex's hand." She looked up at
the ceiling for a few seconds, then turned to Alex and said, "Inside,
you will find not one but two live beetle larvae!" She motioned
for him to cut the gall open, and everyone gasped when Alex
showed the milky-colored larvae inside.

"Sophie, put that away," Ava whispered urgently, while everyone was busy with Alex and the larvae. "We're going to get in
trouble."

Sophie glanced up at the front of the room. Mrs. Ruppert
was busy trying to teach Annika Rock how to cut open a gall
without slicing the larva in half. "No, we're not. Come on." She
held the pencil out to Ava and whispered, "You do it. It's fun!"

Ava shook her head. "Put it away. We shouldn't—"

"Sophie, do your psychic powers work with everything?"
Leo asked.

"Pretty much," she said. "What do you want to know?"

"Varnway's middle name. He won't tell anybody."

"Dude, she's not gonna guess," Luke Varnway said, "and I'm not telling you. You'd never let me hear the end of it."

"I do not guess. I know." Sophie scribbled on the index card in her hand and announced, "And your middle name is Quackenbush."

She said it quietly, but Leo heard and made sure everyone else did, too. "Quackenbush! No way!" He might have thought Sophie made it up until he saw the look on Luke's face. For a few seconds, his mouth hung open wide enough to catch a hundred goldenrod gall flies. Then Leo burst out laughing, and Luke whirled to face Sophie. "Who told you that?"

She made big, innocent eyes. "No one told me. I just knew."

"Quackenbush? Seriously?" Leo made pretend wings out of his arms and started flapping around making duck sounds.

"Boys!" Mrs. Ruppert glared from her desk.

"Sorry!" Leo called, but he didn't stop quacking; he just quacked more quietly.

"Shut *up!*" Luke hissed. "It was my grandma's maiden name, okay? My parents wanted to honor her family and they didn't figure anybody would ever use it." He glared at Sophie.

"Soph, we have to finish this lab." Ava squeezed through the crowd around the table to try again. "Just give me—"

But Jessica Bainbridge darted in front of her. "Sophie!" she said, then lowered her voice. "Can you tell me if Jason Marzigliano likes me?" Her face was all flushed.

Sophie didn't bother to write that one. "Nope. He doesn't."

"Are you sure?"

"Positive."

"How about Tucker Ulster? He's an eighth grader."

"Sophie, come on," Ava whispered. Things were getting louder at their lab table. Ava was sure Mrs. Ruppert would be swooping in any second. She wasn't as strict as Mr. Farkley, but when she got mad, she had this super-calm voice that was scarier than any yell Ava had ever heard.

"Give me the pencil!" Ava whispered urgently. She held out her hand, but Sophie ignored it and started writing casually while she made a big show of asking the ceiling if the other kid liked Jessica.

"The great goldenrod gall fly spirits say Tucker doesn't know who you are," Sophie told her. "But who knows? Maybe he would like you if he did know."

"Hey, Sophie!" Alex shouted.

"I'm not going to warn you again. Keep your voices at a low working level!" Mrs. Ruppert called, frowning over her glasses.

Ava tried again. "Soph, if we don't get back to work she's going to—"

"Sophie!" Tyler Choe squeezed in front of Ava. "How about using your psychic powers to see where I left my math binder this morning?"

"Hold on a second . . ." Sophie scribbled and gazed at the ceiling. "It's in the garbage can in the gym locker room," she said. "Luke swiped it and dumped it there while you were shooting baskets before school."

Tyler whirled around toward Luke, who held up his hands. "Dude . . . that's not true!"

He was way too loud. Ava looked up in a panic. Mrs. Ruppert was coming, and she did not look happy.

Ava held out her hand urgently. "Sophie, give me the pencil!"

"You're such a jerk!" Tyler stepped toward Luke. "My homework was in there and now it's late and—"

"Is there a problem?" Mrs. Ruppert stood glaring at them, hands on her hips.

"Yeah, there's a problem." Tyler pointed to Luke. "Luke *Quackenbush* Varnway threw out my homework."

"I did not and don't call me that!" Luke pointed at Sophie. "*She* started all this!"

Ava watched Mrs. Ruppert's eyes settle on Sophie. And then, on the bright blue pencil in her hand.

11

SHARPENING AND SHORTENING

The pencil wasn't glowing or shooting out sparks or doing other magical things, but it might as well have been, the way Mrs. Ruppert was looking at it. *She knows,* Ava thought, and her heart squeezed up into her throat. *She totally knows and it's my pencil and all my fault and now we're going to be sent to the office and expelled and whatever else happens when you're messing around with a magic pencil instead of doing your goldenrod gall lab.*

Why couldn't Sophie have listened to her? Ava swallowed hard and hoped she'd make it to the office trash can before she threw up, because puking on the goldenrod galls would only make things worse.

But Sophie just smiled. "Sorry, Mrs. Ruppert." She casually dropped the pencil on the lab table. Ava could barely breathe, but she forced herself to reach out and pick it up while Mrs. Ruppert was looking the other way.

"I guess our group got a little off task," Sophie went on. "But this is a great lab. We found one gall with *two* beetle larvae in it. Leo, can you show her?"

Leo stopped quacking at Luke and started looking for the double-larvae gall while Ava hurried to her backpack and zipped the pencil inside. She looked over at the lab table, where Sophie was asking Mrs. Ruppert something about the wasps. Ava still felt like her heart might bound right out of her chest and go thumping across the floor of the science room. How could Sophie be over there chatting like nothing even happened? But at least Mrs. Ruppert was focused on bugs again, and the pencil was safe.

There was barely time to clean up their lab stations before the bell rang. Sophie was waiting for Ava to walk to lunch. "Sorry. I hope you're not mad."

"I'm not mad," Ava said, even though she kind of was. "But we can't do stuff like that."

"Why not?" Sophie stopped at her locker. "Nobody knows it was the pencil."

"But Jessica was all upset and Luke was mad and Tyler wanted to punch him and then Mrs. Ruppert came over and asked if there was a problem and I thought I was going to pass out and I just . . . I want to be careful how we use it, that's all."

"Okay." Sophie twirled out her combination and opened her locker. "Will you bring it to lunch, though?"

"No." It came out louder than Ava intended, but this pencil

was really starting to stress her out. "I want to leave it in my locker for now. I'm going to Mrs. Galvin's Chocolate Chip Cookie Club thing anyway. Want to come?"

"Sure." Sophie didn't seem upset about being snapped at. "If there are cookies, I'm in."

They got their lunches and headed for the library. Ava wished it wasn't a club day so she could shelve books. She needed some quiet to recover from the awful pencil-psychic-science-class scene. And she needed control of her pencil back.

"Sophie, we need to set up rules for this thing, okay?"

"Like what?"

"Like not using it in front of people like you just did. And no more quiz answers. It's cheating."

"But there's no rule against—"

"Only because nobody knows about magic pencils."

Sophie sighed. "Fine. But we can use it for *some* stuff, right?"

Ava nodded. "But only for good stuff, okay? Like to help people."

"Does people include us? Because I saw these super-cute boots at the mall, and I'd love to ask it when they're scheduled to go on sale." Sophie grinned and held open the library door.

Ava laughed. "I think that's okay."

"Hi, girls!" Mrs. Galvin waved toward the tables that were already filling in. "Take a cookie and find a seat."

They did, and then Mrs. Galvin passed out the poem for the day, "Always Bring a Pencil."

Sophie nudged Ava. "See?" she whispered. "Even the poem thinks you should have brought it."

But this poem wasn't about magic. The poet, Naomi Shihab Nye, was saying that certain things—quiet things—*wanted* to be written about in pencil instead of pen. Ava had never thought about that. The poet must not have had teachers who required one or the other.

Then Mrs. Galvin read another poem called "Valentine for Ernest Mann," which wasn't about a valentine at all but about poems and where they hide, where to find them. Ava liked that one, too. It was fun to imagine a poem creeping across her ceiling like sunlight coming through the window.

"So think about that, and if you find a poem hiding somewhere, bring it next time, okay?" Mrs. Galvin said as the bell rang. "Ava, you have a study hall next, right? Do you have time to shelve some new books?"

"Sure." Ava said good-bye to Sophie and rolled a cart of books to the shelf.

Ava always loved ogling new books. Sometimes, she sniffed them when no one was looking. Today, there were a few mysteries that looked pretty good, two books with people kissing on the cover—Ava didn't bother reading the blurbs for those—a bunch of fantasy titles, some nonfiction about the Civil War, and a book called *What to Do When You Worry Too Much: A Kids' Guide to Overcoming Anxiety.*

Ava arranged most of them on the shelves, but she saved the

worry book for last. Its cover had an illustration of a giant tomato plant that looked like it was about to eat a scared-looking kid standing next to it. Ava glanced back at the circulation desk and saw that Mrs. Galvin was doing something on her computer. She opened the book to see what the killer tomatoes were all about. The first chapter said that worries were like plants, that if you mostly kept busy and ignored them, they tended to wither and get smaller. But if you fed and watered them and gave them lots of attention, they'd grow big and healthy. Only worries weren't healthy, the book said.

No kidding, Ava thought. She put it on the shelf, grabbed her backpack, and waved to Mrs. Galvin. "See you next week!"

The second that school ended, Ava and Sophie hurried home and up to Ava's bedroom. "Here you go." Ava handed Sophie the pencil. Sophie scribbled: When are the boots I like at the mall going on sale? and waited. Then she sighed.

"What?" Ava asked. "They're not going on sale?"

"It's not answering. Maybe the pencil doesn't like shopping." Sophie let out a huff and tossed the pencil over her shoulder. It landed on the hardwood floor and rolled under Ava's bed.

"Hey, be careful!" Ava hurried over, pulled the pencil out from under the bed, and blew off a dust bunny. "You broke the tip."

"Sorry," Sophie said. "You have a sharpener, right?"

Ava nodded and took the pencil over to the sharpener on

her bookshelf. She stuck it in and started sharpening. She could feel the pencil vibrating, getting shorter as the blades chewed away at the wood. Getting shorter . . .

Ava gasped and stopped sharpening. "Sophie, we have to stop asking so many questions. Even the good, helpful ones." She pulled it out and blew wood shavings off the sharpened tip. "Every time we sharpen it, it shrinks, and when it's gone . . ."

Sophie's eyes got big. "Ohmygosh, I totally didn't think of that. I figured once we knew it wasn't a genie-with-three-wishes thing, we were good." She stared at the pencil. "How long do you think it'll last if we ask it, like, ten questions a day?"

"I'm not sure." Marcus would probably have some math formula or algorithm to figure that out, but she could only take a wild guess. "How long does a regular pencil last?"

"Ask the pencil that." Sophie pointed to it.

Ava hesitated. "Couldn't we find that out somewhere else?"

"Good point. New rule: never use the pencil for a question unless Google doesn't know the answer."

They went downstairs, where Google told them the average pencil can write about forty-five thousand words. "But those words could go by fast." Ava did some quick math on a napkin someone left by the phone. "We've had the pencil less than a week, and we've already asked it more than thirty questions. Plus it wasn't new when I got it—it'd been used a bunch already. What if we go with three questions a day for now?"

"Perfect," Sophie said, reaching for her purse. "Do you think we could use one more question today? Please?" Sophie batted her eyelashes, which made Ava laugh.

"Fine."

Sophie grinned. "I think this particular question may work best if we're at the mall. Think your dad or Gram would give us a ride?"

12

THE BOOT WHISPERERS

Erdman's Shoe Shop was Sophie's favorite place in the universe. She practically danced down the aisle to the boots she'd been stalking. "Okay, ready?"

Ava sat down on the shoe-trying bench and flipped to a clean yellow page of her legal pad, pencil poised. "Yep. Go ahead."

Sophie read the boot brand, size, and color from the side of the box. Ava got it all down. "Double-check it before I add the question mark so we don't waste this one." Ava held up the legal pad.

When will the size 7 Tony Lama Mosto brown boots with the fringe go on sale at Erdman's Shoe Shop at the Lakeview Mall

Sophie nodded. "That should work."

Ava started to add the question mark, but Sophie grabbed her hand. "Hold on!"

"What?"

"Can you ask how much of a discount it'll be in the same question?"

Ava hesitated. "What if it gets mad that we're trying to sneak two questions into one?"

Sophie looked at the pencil. "I don't think it'll care. It's a matter of saving the lead. We're being responsible. Like when my mom runs two or three errands in one trip to save gas."

That sounded like the sort of thing the pencil would approve of, so Ava added the part about the discount, scribbled a question mark, and waited.

"Good news," she told Sophie. "They'll be fifty percent off on Sunday."

"Perfect! I'll have Dad bring me this weekend." She put the boots back on the shelf, then wandered down the aisle, picking up ballet flats and bright-colored sneakers. "Ava!" Her face lit up. "We should open a business! We can be personal shoppers and advise people on what to wear and when to buy the stuff, and they'll save tons of money. It'll be the coolest thing ever!" Sophie's voice kept getting louder, and customers were starting to stare, but she didn't seem to notice. "Everybody's going to want to hire us! We can advertise . . . I don't know . . . somewhere . . . and maybe they'll even do a story about us in *Teen Vogue* and—"

"Shh!" Ava put a hand on Sophie's arm. "Soph, take a deep breath."

Sophie stopped talking and was quiet for a few seconds.

She sighed. "I guess that's not entirely realistic. But this is so much *fun*."

"Maybe we can help people, even if we're not going into business. Look." Ava pointed to another woman who was trying on the boots Sophie liked.

The woman got one boot on before her toddler took off, and she had to run limping along after him. She led him back to the bench and caught Ava's eye. "Remind me not to go boot shopping with Timothy again." She pulled on the second boot and looked in the mirror. "What do you think?" she asked Ava and Sophie. "Can I pull these off?"

"They look great," Ava said, then added in a quieter voice, "but if you're going to buy them, you might want to wait until Sunday. They're going to be fifty percent off."

The woman's face lit up. "How did you find out? They're so tight-lipped about sales here."

"We know somebody," Ava said. It was close enough to the truth.

Ava and Sophie decided the fun of saving strangers money was worth breaking their three-questions-a-day rule. They skulked around the store like spies, watching to see who was serious about a purchase before scribbling questions and then approaching with the good news.

"All those sneakers are going to be half price next week," Ava whispered to a woman shopping for her sons.

"If you come back on Monday," Sophie told another lady, "those red flats will be twenty percent off."

"Thank you." The woman tipped her head. "Do you two work here?"

"No." Sophie smiled mysteriously. "We just know things."

***

Ava had never loved shopping like Sophie did, but today, she could have stayed for hours. She couldn't stop smiling as they ate their frozen yogurt, waiting for Gram to pick them up. "That was the best mall day ever."

"I know, right?" Sophie licked her spoon.

"I wish everybody in the world could be as happy as that lady was when she found out the sneakers weren't going to cost eighty dollars." Ava thought about all the tired faces at Cedar Bay, faces like Grandpa's that could use some happiness. She pulled the pencil from her pocket. "Sophie, I know what we can do next."

"Let me guess. Lottery numbers? No . . . it'll say the dumb lottery ball lady has free will when she reaches into that spinny thing. Maybe . . ."

"Better than that," Ava said. "Let's take the pencil to visit my grandpa's nursing home after school on Monday!"

13

UNSPOKEN SECRETS OF CEDAR BAY

"I should have told my parents we were coming," Ava said. But Mom and Dad had been busy working on Saturday, and Sunday was Halloween, so the doorbell kept ringing every time Ava started to bring it up. It felt weird to be walking to Cedar Bay instead of riding in the van.

"It's not like they'd say no. You're visiting your grandfather." Sophie pulled the door open and they headed down the hall. "Besides, it's easier to be forgiven than it is to get permission. That's like the number-one life rule."

Ava laughed. "Maybe for you." Ava's number-one rule was more like "Always check on everything to make sure you never get in trouble because that would be the worst thing ever." But if Mom knew about this visit, she probably would have come, too, and then Ava and Sophie wouldn't have been able to carry out their secret pencil wish-granting mission.

"Come on in, girls!" Betty, one of the nurses, waved them into the community room. "Sneaking in an extra visit this week?" She parked Mrs. Yu's wheelchair next to Mrs. Raymond.

"We brought Ava's grandpa some music," Sophie said. They'd loaded Sophie's iPod with pretty much everything they could find—Sophie and Ava's popular rock, Marcus's moody classical stuff, Mr. Anderson's country songs, Mrs. Anderson's modern jazz, and a song by a Moroccan band that Sophie's dad liked. It reminded Ava of the belly dancers she'd seen at the county fair once.

"Good luck with that. He's in a mood today." Betty looked down the hallway. Thomas, one of the assistants, was wheeling a scowling Grandpa toward dinner.

"Hi, Grandpa!" Ava said.

Grandpa grunted. Ava leaned over and gave him a quick kiss on the cheek once his wheelchair was parked. Dad always told her that even on bad days, the old Grandpa was still in there somewhere, under all the wrinkles and sourness, and he might appreciate a kiss even if Grump-Grandpa didn't.

"We brought you some music." Sophie held up her iPod. Then she turned to Ava and whispered, "Ask the pencil what we should play."

Ava pulled the pencil and her legal pad from her backpack and wrote:

What song should we play for Grandpa?

"It didn't answer," Ava told Sophie.

"Ask it why not."

Ava did, and the pencil-voice replied, "Because it is not my job to give advice on playing DJ for a grumpy old man."

"Wow." Ava put the pencil down and repeated what it said to Sophie. "I don't think the pencil likes Grandpa."

"It only does facts, remember? Ask it . . ." Sophie thought for a second. "What is Grandpa's favorite kind of music?"

Ava did that, and the pencil-voice said, "Jazz."

"Jazz," Ava repeated.

"Perfect!" Sophie searched until she found one of Mrs. Anderson's jazz songs. "I think you'll like this one." She eased the buds into Grandpa's ears and pressed Play.

Grandpa blew a grouchy puff of air through his cracked lips and batted the bud out of his right ear.

"Or not." Sophie took her earbuds back. Thomas showed up and set plates of mushy-looking lasagna in front of Grandpa and Mrs. Grabowski, and they started eating.

"You want some dessert, girls?" Thomas asked. "I think I can sneak you a couple of Jell-O or pudding cups."

"No thanks," Ava said, watching Grandpa eat his lasagna and move on to the wiggly green Jell-O. Mrs. Grabowski left hers on the plate and pushed it away. "She looks sad today," Ava whispered to Sophie.

Sophie shrugged. "See if she wants to hear some music."

So Ava wrote: Does Mrs. Grabowski want to hear some music?

"Not particularly," the pencil-voice answered.

Ava paused, then wrote: What does Mrs. Grabowski want right now?

"She wants to go back to Ukraine and dance like she did when she was a girl," the voice said.

Ava looked at Mrs. Grabowski hunched over the table. There wasn't much chance of that working out.

But then the voice said, "Also, she wants pudding instead of Jell-O."

Ava told Sophie about Mrs. Grabowski's wishes.

"The Jell-O thing's way easier," Sophie said. So when Thomas came back, Ava pointed to Mrs. Grabowski. "Could she have pudding instead?"

Thomas tipped his head, confused. "How come? She looks like she's done eating."

"Just see if she wants some, okay? Please?" Sophie smiled.

Thomas laughed. "I think you're the one who's after the pudding—but that's fine. I'll see if there's some left."

He came back with a cup of vanilla pudding and put it down next to Mrs. Grabowski's abandoned Jell-O. She pulled her tray closer and started eating.

"Well, how about that." Thomas looked at Ava and Sophie. "You two got some secret you want to let me in on?"

Ava panicked for a second, but Sophie laughed. "We just pay attention to things."

Then Mr. Clemson hollered from across the room, "I smell smoke! Call for backup!" Thomas left to reassure him that it was only a batch of overdone cookies coming out of the oven.

Ava looked around the room, at all of the faces with faraway eyes. "What do you think the rest of them are thinking?"

Sophie grinned. "We know how to find out."

They went from table to table, all over the dining room.

What does Mr. Ames want?

"More lasagna," the voice said. So Ava got Betty to bring him another portion.

"Also a baseball," the voice added.

"A baseball?" Ava said. The voice didn't repeat itself.

"What's he going to do with a baseball?" Sophie asked.

Ava shrugged. It didn't seem worth spending the lead to ask the pencil why he wanted it when it was so easy to get for him. Sophie pulled out a pen and wrote "Mr. Ames—Baseball" on the legal pad so they'd remember to bring one next time.

What does Mr. Clemson want?

"A pick head axe, an attack hose, and a truck with an aerial ladder," the voice said.

"Oh dear. He wants a fire truck, a hose, and an axe," Ava told Sophie. She looked up at Mr. Clemson, who was gesturing urgently toward the window, insisting that Thomas smash it so they could all climb out.

Sophie shook her head. "Tell the pencil to try again."

Ava wrote: What does Mr. Clemson want that will fit in this room and can't be used to break, smash, or flood things?

"Wool socks," the voice said. That was better. Ava wrote "Mr. Clemson—Socks" and moved on.

What does Mrs. Raymond want?

"A new sweatshirt," the voice said. Ava told Sophie.

"Really?" Sophie said. "She has so many. See what color she wants—and what animals she doesn't have yet."

What color would Mrs. Raymond like her sweatshirt to be, and what kind of animal would she like on it?

"It doesn't matter what color," the voice said, "but *no* stupid animals. That's all her kids ever give her for holidays and she hates them."

"Oh," Ava said, and repeated the answer to Sophie.

Sophie nodded. "No wonder she wants a new one."

Ava added Mrs. Raymond's koala-and-kitten-free sweatshirt to the list and moved to the next table with Mrs. Yu.

What does Mrs. Yu want?

"Hmph. She wants to sit by your grandfather," the voice said. It didn't sound happy about that.

Ava looked over at Grandpa. He was scowling at his Jell-O.

Really? she wrote. Why?

"Because she thinks he's handsome," the voice said. "But don't tell him that. It'll go straight to his head."

Ava looked at her grandfather and tried to see what Mrs. Yu saw. Grandpa was all slouched over and grouchy-faced. His short white hair against the dark skin of his head made it look as if he'd been out in the snow. Handsome?

"What?" Sophie's voice was impatient.

"She wants to go sit by Grandpa."

"Ha!" Sophie laughed but she didn't ask why. She squatted down next to Mrs. Yu and said, "We're going to change tables, okay?" Then she grabbed the handles of Mrs. Yu's wheelchair and relocated her next to Grandpa.

Grandpa looked up, surprised, but he didn't frown. He nodded and went back to his Jell-O.

Ava looked at her watch. "We should go," she said. "I need to get home for dinner." The pencil was fun here, but Ava still felt sad about Mrs. Grabowski. Her pudding was gone, and she wasn't going to Ukraine any time soon.

"What about your grandfather?" Sophie asked.

"It'll probably say he wants us to go away," Ava said. But she sat down and wrote:

What does Grandpa want?

Ava listened to the pencil's answer, then told Sophie, "He wants to see Johnny Hodges in concert."

"Who's that?"

"No idea." Ava wrote down the name. "Why don't we look him up online? We can see if he's touring anywhere nearby, and then—"

"But more than that," the pencil-voice interrupted, "he wants your mother's forgiveness."

14

ELECTION NIGHT ANGST

He wants your mother's forgiveness.

For what? Ava hadn't had time to ask the pencil at the nursing home because she and Sophie had been running late. And then she decided she probably *shouldn't* ask, since they were trying not to use up questions. She could ask her mom what happened later. Mom wasn't like the Cedar Bay people who couldn't talk for themselves.

All through classes on Tuesday, Ava thought about what the pencil said. She decided she'd ask Mom about it after school. But the sounds that greeted Ava when she opened the front door told her that wasn't a good idea. It was a blend of TV news, angry dishwasher unloading, and her mother's voice.

"The man has been serving in the Senate twelve *years* and they decide *now* they need to study his college discipline records?" Mom thumped a mug onto the shelf over the sink, then pulled out the silverware thing and started shoving forks into the drawer. *Clink. Clink. Clink!* "Today of all days!" *Clink! Clink!* "Bunch of desperate mudslingers." She slammed the drawer closed and turned back to the dishwasher. All that was left were the wineglasses. They were doomed.

Dad stepped in and rescued them. "How about if I get these?" He reached for a glass. "Hi, Ava. How was school?"

"Pretty good."

Mom walked over and flicked off the TV. "I shouldn't even bother voting tonight."

"Well, I haven't been to the polls yet. If I stay home, you won't feel the need to go and cancel out my vote." Dad put away the last wineglass and closed the dishwasher. "What if we let this campaign season end early and call it a night?" He reached for Mom's hand, but she shoved it into an oven mitt and pulled out the garlic bread.

"That's fine." She let out a huff of a sigh. "I have a lot of paperwork to catch up on anyway." Then she turned to Ava. "Why are you home so late? Were jazz tryouts today?"

"Not until next week. Where's everybody else?"

"Let's see." Dad ticked off family members on his fingers. "Emma is at Emma P's house for a playdate and pizza. Marcus is doing homework, and Gram's taking a nap."

"Again?"

"She's just slowing down a little, Ava. She'll be seventy-five next month, you know."

"I know." Ava hated that. She was already feeling sad from being at Cedar Bay. Why did more people she loved have to get old?

Dinner was quiet without Emma. Gram came down, but she mostly pushed her food around on her plate. Marcus didn't have much to say either. It seemed like he'd left his brain up in his room to work on physics problems and just sent his body downstairs for chicken and mashed potatoes. Mom kept looking at her watch.

"So listen," Dad said. "What do you think about world-famous donuts?"

"What's special about donuts?" Ava asked.

"Nothing," Mom said. Her plate was still half-full, but she stood up and took it to the sink.

Ava felt bad for her dad. "I bet you could come up with a cool donut."

"You think?" Dad said. "There's a place in Richland, Washington, called the Spudnut Shop. They make donuts with potato flour. Get it? *Spud*nut? It's great, right?"

"It's interesting." Ava poked at her mashed potatoes. They didn't seem like they'd be good in a donut, but you never knew. Frosting made most things okay.

"Or maybe we could have the world's *biggest* donuts," Dad said. "A place called Round Rock Donuts advertises a Texas-size donut that's bigger than your face. We could do something like that only bigger."

"And advertise it as a heart attack with a hole in the center," Mom called from the sink.

Marcus laughed at that, but Ava saw her father's face fall.

"We're out of dish soap." Mom grabbed her keys from the counter. "I'm going to run up to Champlain Market and grab some other groceries, too. Anybody need anything else?"

"Nope, I think we're good." Dad started clearing plates. Ava put away the salt and pepper shakers, and nobody said anything else about giant donuts.

Ava wanted to ask Dad what would happen to the store if none of the new publicity ideas worked. What if it had to close when the new superstore opened? And if it did, what would Dad do for a job? But her dad already seemed deflated, and she didn't want to make it worse. "I'm going to do my homework."

"Me, too." Marcus left for his room.

Dad looked at the clock. "I might take a walk in a little bit. It's nice out, and I could use some air. If I do, I won't be long."

Ava took her backpack and saxophone up to her bedroom and closed the door. She knew she should start her homework, but she had that icky feeling in her stomach that she always got when her parents were short with each other. She'd already asked the pencil if they were getting divorced and gotten that dumb lecture about free will. They probably still hadn't had time to go see a lawyer, but what if they were thinking about it?

Ava wished she knew more about what made people get

divorced. Those divorced people were probably nothing like her parents. She was probably worried for no reason at all. She took out the blue pencil and wrote:

Why do people get divorced?

The pencil didn't answer. It was a dumb question, Ava realized. People probably had all different reasons. She tried being more specific:

Why did Sophie's parents get divorced?

"Because Sophie's dad started spending time with a woman from his office and fell in love with her."

Ava gasped. Sophie had told her about Jenna, but never that she was the reason for the divorce. Did Sophie even know?

Does Sophie know that?

"No."

That made sense. Ava remembered when Sophie first found out about the divorce. Sophie said her parents sat her down in the living room on a Saturday morning and said they loved her but they weren't in love with each other anymore. They must have left out the part about Sophie's dad loving somebody else.

Ava thought about calling Sophie to tell her, but she didn't think she'd want to know if it had been one of her parents. She felt bad enough knowing about Sophie's dad and kind of wished she could un-ask that question.

Ava dropped the pencil in the desk drawer, popped a reed in her mouth, and put together her saxophone. She ran through some scales to warm up and played the *Titanic* song. It would have been pretty if she hadn't seen the movie. But now she knew it was about icebergs and death and drowning, so she couldn't like it, no matter how much Miss Romero wanted her to play it.

Ava tried Miss Romero's song again, too—the frantic one the pencil said she liked. Ava had to slow it down a lot to get the right notes, and it sounded stupid that way. She put her saxophone down and flipped through the other music. It all looked too hard, or too slow and sad.

Ava flopped the music onto her desk and saw her notes from the nursing home again. At the bottom was the name of the musician from Grandpa's first wish: Johnny Hodges.

She went back to the kitchen. "Okay if I look something up on the computer?"

"Sure." Her dad had the TV on. The newspeople were starting to guess which candidate would win Ohio.

Ava sat down and saw she had an email from Sophie. The subject line had Jason Marzigliano's name with a bunch of exclamation points and little hearts made out of less-than signs and threes. The body was a single run-on sentence. When Sophie was excited, punctuation was the first thing to go.

OMG Jason was at gymnastics when I got there and he said hi to me and I said hi back before he went over to the vault but then all I could think about was what the pencil said and I was just like EEEEEEEEEE and so I might ask him to go out with me soon so I don't have to wait!!!!

Ava smiled. Sophie's crazy energy was contagious some-times. She closed the email, typed "Johnny Hodges" in the search box, and found out right away that Grandpa's wish wasn't going to work out. Johnny Hodges was a jazz musician who had died in 1970. Grandpa must have heard him play a long, long time ago. But not before the days of video cameras, apparently, because one of the search results was a link to a video. Ava clicked on it.

Johnny Hodges actually looked a little like Grandpa, with bushy eyebrows and a scruffy mustache. He had more hair, though, and his hadn't turned white when this video was taken back in the 1960s. He played alto saxophone, like Ava.

Scoo-ba-doo-ba-doo-wahhh . . .

Only not like Ava. Johnny Hodges's sound was mellow and smooth, as if the music that poured out of his horn had never had a worry in its life. "On the Sunny Side of the Street," the song was called, and Johnny Hodges played it with his whole body, like the music was working itself right up from his toes and he just had to move a little to bring it out.

Bwahhh-ba-doo-be-doo-wooo . . .

Ava left the video running and opened another window to see if she could find the sheet music.

"Hey, Dad . . . If I give you two dollars, can I use your credit card to buy music for this song?"

"Sure." Dad was still glued to the election coverage. He pulled out his wallet and waved the card in her direction.

Ava downloaded the song, printed it, and went back to her room. She didn't sound like Johnny Hodges when she was sight-reading the piece, but she didn't sound bad either. She wondered if maybe a little of that chilled-out feeling was getting out of the song and into her.

Right when she was taking a breath, she heard the kitchen door close and stopped to listen for Mom's voice. She hoped her parents wouldn't start arguing about the election again. But it was quiet.

Ava looked out her window and saw her dad walking down the sidewalk in the streetlight. She looked at her alarm clock. It was a quarter of nine. Late to be going for a walk.

Ava's eyes fell on the paper with her questions about Sophie's dad and the answer about why he'd left his family, and her stomach twisted. Ava liked Mr. Chafik. He loved to sing and laugh, and he was funny like her dad. How could somebody so nice do something like that?

And Sophie hadn't known a thing about it. Ava looked out the window at her father, hurrying along in the streetlight, and a big, awful what-if rushed into her gut and squeezed out every last note of calm. She grabbed the pencil.

Where is my dad going right now?

It didn't answer. Stupid, stupid, stupid free will! Ava slammed the pencil down on the desk.

What if he wasn't just going for a walk? What if he was using his dumb free will to go somewhere else, to see somebody who wasn't her mom so he could fall in love with her? Ava felt like she'd eaten way too much sugary junk food. Her heart was racing, and her stomach hurt, and she *knew* she was being ridiculous, but she couldn't make her body stop feeling awful and couldn't make her head stop thinking those things, so she raced downstairs, threw on her sneakers, and went outside.

"*Mehhh!*" Lucy yelled at her, but Ava forced herself to be still. She waited, holding the screen door behind her so it wouldn't slam. Then she raced down the steps and squinted into the dark. Her father was at the end of the block. If he was just out for a quick walk, he'd turn right and do the loop they always did on their bikes—the one that went past the park. That's what he would do. He'd turn right and loop around the block by the park and come home where he belonged. Ava held her breath and waited for him to turn right.

He turned left.

So she raced down the block after him.

15

IN THE DEAD OF NIGHT

Ava flew to the corner, then paused and peered down Maple Street. Her dad was walking down the sidewalk whistling—*whistling!*—as if taking a walk in the dark was a perfectly normal thing for him to be doing. He went past the market, crossed Champlain Avenue, and kept walking. Where was he *going?* Ava followed him, keeping her distance, staying in the shadows.

Finally, her dad slowed down and turned into the driveway to—the fire station? Why would he be going there?

And then she remembered it wasn't just a fire station today. It was a polling place. Her mouth dropped open.

"Dad!"

He whirled around and held up his hands. "Ava! What are you doing here?"

"What are *you* doing here?" Ava pointed to the campaign signs that lined the sidewalk. Her voice shook, but the words spilled out. "You're *voting*! How could you? You made a deal with Mom. You promised!"

"I just . . . I was watching the news, and—"

"Evening, Rich!" Mr. Varnway called as he headed to his car. "You and Alisha trying to be the last two votes before they count 'em?"

"Just me tonight, Ed."

"Oh, no, she's here." Mr. Varnway pointed to the fire station. Yellow light poured from the open door. "Saw her in line on my way out. You two are ships that pass in the night, eh?" He chuckled and waved and got into his Jeep.

Ava looked at her dad. "Did . . . did you guys change your mind and decide you'd vote after all?"

"No." He pressed his lips together, looked at the lit-up door, and then turned back to Ava grinning. "Come with me! We're going to surprise Mom." He took off running toward the door, and Ava followed, but she had a pit in her stomach that felt like it was in the process of growing into a whole, humongous avocado. Was he going to confront Mom right here? If they got into a fight right in front of everybody . . .

"Over here. Shhh!" Dad waved for Ava to hide at the side of the door, pressed against the building as if they were on some kind of police stakeout.

Her mom's voice drifted out of the building. "Well, tell Raymond I said hello and I hope he's feeling better. Have a good night."

High-heeled footsteps clicked across the floor, and just as they got to the door, Ava's dad jumped in front of it. "Nice night for democracy, isn't it?"

Ava's mom jumped about a mile and then just stood there, eyes huge, staring at her dad.

Ava was blinking like crazy. She wanted to hide. She wanted to crawl between the cracks in the bricks like an ant so she wouldn't have to see them argue. No, she wanted to run—to run away and keep running so she wouldn't have to hear them either. But her feet felt cemented to the sidewalk, and she couldn't go anywhere, so she braced herself for the worst.

Her dad burst out laughing.

Big, loud belly laughs.

And then her mom laughed, too. "How did you *know*?"

"I was ... I was ..." Her dad was laughing so hard he couldn't catch his breath, and the voting-place volunteers were starting to stare.

Mom's eyes got even bigger. "You didn't know, did you?! You came to vote, too, you stinker!" She shook her head, then held out her arms, and Dad wrapped her up in a big hug.

Ava stared. They didn't look like they were about to get divorced, but the pencil would probably say you could never tell about these things. Free will and everything. Still, she couldn't help feeling a little better.

"Come on, Ava." Her dad held one arm open. "Family hug, and then you can come with me to cancel out Mom's vote."

Ava went into the booth with her dad and helped him fill in the little bubbles while her mom waited. Then Ava slipped her dad's ballot into the counting machine, and they left. Ava still felt full of nervous prickles, but neither of her parents seemed mad on the walk, so she tried not to worry.

It was past nine when they got home. Dad went to say good night to Emma, but Ava stayed in the kitchen while Mom started the dishes.

"At least you really did get dish soap," Ava said, reaching for a towel to dry. "So it wasn't a total lie."

Mom sighed and squirted some soap into the sink. A few bubbles floated up toward the ceiling. "How much have I damaged your image of me tonight?"

Ava thought about that. "Not much," she said. If Dad wasn't mad, she figured it was okay. "But I'm never going to forget the look on your face when Dad jumped out at you."

Mom laughed and handed Ava a plate to dry. "Never is a mighty long time."

Ava smiled. That was a quote from *Peter Pan*, almost. As usual, Mom had made up her own version. "It's supposed to be an *awfully* long time," Ava told her. "It was also an *awfully* funny expression on your face, so I think it's fair to say I'll never forget." She wiped off the plate and slid it onto the pile in the cupboard. "Hey, Mom . . . I was wondering about something."

"What's that?"

"Why don't you and Grandpa talk very much?"

"Grandpa doesn't talk much to anybody." Mom held out a handful of dripping silverware.

"Yeah, but . . . it seems like . . ." Ava dried the forks and spoons and put them away. She should have planned this conversation better. It wasn't like she could tell Mom what the pencil said. "I don't know. It just seems like maybe you're mad at him or something."

"Nope." Mom ran some more hot water into the sink. "We just don't see things the same way." She turned off the water, reached over with her sudsy hands, and gave Ava a quick hug. "Get ready for bed, okay? I'll come to read in a bit."

Ava nodded. She'd have to try asking about Grandpa another time. She was tired anyway.

Ava went upstairs and changed into her pajamas. She was on her way to brush her teeth when she heard music coming from the kitchen. Jazz music. Ava figured her parents would be watching election results on TV, but this sounded like that Johnny Hodges song she'd found online earlier.

She crouched at the top of the stairs in her pajamas and peered through the spindles on the railing. The TV was off. But there was Johnny Hodges, playing on the computer screen again, all *da-ba-doo-ba-doo-wahhh-wahhh*, with his eyes half closed, lost in the music, while his drummer grooved away behind him.

And there were her parents—her father, holding her mother close, Mom's tight black curls tucked under the blond-gray stubble on Dad's chin. They were smiling. Dancing while the soapsuds sat in the sink.

Ava brushed her teeth, went to her room, and picked up the pencil.

Are Mom and Dad really okay with each other and as happy as they look right now?

"They really are," the voice answered.

This time, Ava believed it.

What's up with Mom and Grandpa?

The pencil didn't answer. Ava figured she'd phrased the question wrong, but she was too tired to try again. At least her parents were happy. The polls were closed, so their big arguing season was over.

Who won the stupid election? Ava wrote.

The pencil answered. Ava wasn't sure when the official results came out, but once they did, Mom wasn't going to be happy for long.

16

MUSIC, MONSTER TRUCKS, AND TIARAS

"Has anybody seen my physics textbook?" Marcus said, rummaging through papers on the kitchen counter.

"Check the living room," Gram told him. "I think I saw it in there."

"I can't believe we have this yahoo in charge of the country for another four years." Ava's mom shoved the newspaper across the kitchen table to make room for a plate of toast.

"Four more years . . . four more years . . ." Dad walked past, chanting as if he were at one of those post-election victory parties. Mom rolled up the front page and swatted him on the butt. He laughed and pulled her into a hug, and Ava thought that was probably a good sign they wouldn't be at the lawyer's office today either.

"It's not there," Marcus said. "I need that book."

"Try the stairs," Mom told him.

"I've been thinking about giant fruits and vegetables," Dad said, grabbing an apple from the bowl on the table. "Maybe we could grow a world-famous cucumber or something in that plot out back."

"Since when are you a gardener?" Mom pulled the orange juice from the fridge. "I couldn't even get you to help weed the tomatoes last summer."

"Yeah, but if they were *giant* tomatoes, I'd have been all over that."

"Then we could make a giant pizza!" Emma-My-Name-Is-Electron said.

Marcus stared at her name tag. "Did you take my physics book?"

"Oh! Maybe." Emma-My-Name-Is-Electron ran upstairs and came down with Marcus's book. There were about a dozen colored slips of paper sticking out among the pages. "Can you leave the sticky notes in there? Your book has good names."

"We're going to family night at Cedar Bay later, right?" Ava asked, reaching for a banana.

"Ugh, it's Wednesday, isn't it?" Her mom sighed.

"Do you guys know what the entertainment is tonight?" Ava asked. "If it's nothing too long, maybe I could bring my saxophone." She'd been thinking about what the pencil said . . . what Grandpa wanted. Mom's forgiveness wasn't something Ava could give him, especially when she didn't know what he needed to be forgiven for. She wasn't about to ask, at least not until her mother got over being mad about having a yahoo in the White House. And she couldn't bring a dead saxophonist back to life either. But she could remind Grandpa of the music he'd loved. "I've been practicing a song I think Grandpa will like."

"That would be great," Dad said.

"Don't take it personally if he's in one of his moods," Mom added.

"I won't." Ava thought about her trip to Cedar Bay with Sophie and the list they'd made. "Do we have any old baseballs around?"

"Maybe." Dad frowned and looked up at the ceiling. "There might be some in the garage from Marcus's Little League days. Over in the corner with those old tennis rackets."

"I'll check on my way out. Thanks!" Ava threw away her banana peel, grabbed her backpack and saxophone, and headed to the garage. She found half a dozen cobwebby baseballs on a low shelf, brushed off two newish-looking balls and one older one, put them in her backpack, and started down the driveway to meet Sophie.

"*Mehhh!*" Ethel yelled. Ava jumped about a mile and then ran the rest of the way to the sidewalk, even though the goats were fenced in.

"Look what I found for Mrs. Raymond!" Sophie dropped her backpack, unzipped it, and pulled out a black sweatshirt with gray-and-red lettering that said METAL EATERS: MONSTER TRUCK XTREME!! above a picture of a truck with pointy teeth.

"Wow. That's no kitten," Ava said. "Do you think she'll like it? It's pretty intense."

"That's the whole point," Sophie said, stuffing it back into her backpack. "She's tired of snuggly kittens. She wants action!"

◄━━━━━▪▫

Ava and Sophie spent every free moment of the school day making plans for family night at Cedar Bay. Besides Mrs. Raymond's monster truck sweatshirt, Sophie had found a pair of thick woolen socks for Mr. Clemson. "And I brought this for Mrs. Grabowski," she whispered across the table in study hall, pulling a big flowery tiara from her backpack.

The flowers weren't real—just plastic—but they were pretty, and a bright stream of multicolored ribbons spilled down the back. Ava reached out to touch them. "Did you make this?"

Sophie nodded. "Remember how she said she wanted to go back to Ukraine and dance? I looked up traditional Ukrainian costumes online and found something like this, so Jenna took me to the craft store and I got stuff to put one together. That means we've got everybody covered except Mrs. Yu—"

"All she wants is to sit by Grandpa, so we can totally do that," Ava said.

"—and your grandpa." Sophie looked at Ava. "Did you talk to your mom?"

"Not really," Ava admitted. "But I'm going to play a Johnny Hodges song for him tonight if there's time. I found the sheet music and practiced and everything."

She'd give Grandpa part of his wish, at least, while she figured out the rest.

17

SPECIAL GUEST

Sophie came over to Ava's house after school to make sure they had the nursing home pencil-wishes ready. On the way to Cedar Bay, they huddled in the backseat, going over their plan. Dad kept interrupting to ask for help brainstorming world-famous ways to save the general store. He was really hopeful about vegetables.

"World's largest pumpkin?"

Marcus poked at his phone. "Taken."

"Potatoes?" Sophie offered up.

"Taken."

"Watermelon?" Dad said, turning into the driveway of Cedar Bay.

That stole Emma-My-Name-Is-Electron's attention from the bracelet she'd been braiding. "Ooh! Let's grow a giant watermelon!"

"We're too far north to grow really big watermelons," Mom said.

"We could go for a world-famous whoopee cushion," Marcus said, getting out of the car. "The world's largest one of those was only about ten feet in diameter."

"Can you imagine the sound that thing would make if you sat on it?" He stuck out his tongue and made a giant, spitty *Ppphhbbbbt* sound in the parking lot, so loud that Mrs. Grabowski's daughter turned and stared. Then she hurried up the sidewalk into the building.

That cracked Sophie up. "Ha! She's running away before the smell reaches her."

When they got inside, Emma and Marcus headed straight for the cookie table. Mom and Dad followed them to make sure Emma didn't swipe the whole platter. Grandpa hadn't come down from his room yet, but Mr. Ames was there, sitting by the window alone.

Ava nudged Sophie and pointed. "Let's give him his baseball." It seemed a good place to start.

"Mr. Ames?" Ava stepped up to his wheelchair, squatted down, and pulled the three baseballs from her backpack. She held them out. "We brought you something."

His head was a little droopy, and for a second, Ava thought Mr. Ames was just going to doze off and ignore them, but then his eyes opened wider and focused on the baseballs in Ava's hands.

"Do you want one? Or all of them? You can have them all if you want." She started to hand him the newest, cleanest looking one, but he reached for the older one instead. It was all scuffed up with dirt and its stitches were fraying, but Mr. Ames pulled it into his lap and looked down at it, just staring.

"Um ... do you want these, too?" She held up the other balls, but Mr. Ames didn't answer. He kept staring at that dirty old baseball in his hands, as if there were secrets stitched into the leather, invisible to everyone but him.

"Okay, then." Ava put the other baseballs back in her backpack, turned to Sophie, and shrugged. "I guess he likes it. You want to find Mrs. Grabowski next? Or Mr. Clemson?"

Sophie looked around the room. Mrs. Grabowski was sitting in her purple pantsuit beside her daughter, waiting for the junior high school quartet to play. Mr. Clemson was by the cookie table, waving away the lemonade Betty was trying to give him, and shouting for his turnout gear. "Let's go see Mrs. Grabowski first," Sophie decided. "If we try to give Mr. Clemson the socks now, he'll be upset we don't have the helmet and jacket, too."

Ava started after Sophie. She glanced back at Mr. Ames by the window just as he lifted the baseball to his nose and took a deep, deep breath. The nursing home air reeked of overcooked vegetables and disinfectant, but Mr. Ames looked like he was smelling roses or warm bread from a bakery, like he was sitting in a ballpark breathing in the scent of newly mown grass. *Maybe he was*, Ava thought. She hoped so.

Ava was nervous about approaching Mrs. Grabowski with her daughter right there, but Sophie didn't have any trouble explaining why she was putting a crazy, multicolored flower-and-ribbon headdress on the old lady's head.

"We heard that she loves Ukrainian music," Sophie told Mrs. Grabowski's daughter, "and I was doing this project at school about . . . um . . . culture. I found out this is what people wore when they danced in Ukraine. So I made one for her."

Mrs. Grabowski's face lit up when she saw the headdress. She pulled the stream of ribbons forward, so they flowed over the shoulder of her purple jacket.

"Do you want to see yourself?" Sophie asked.

Mrs. Grabowski nodded, so Sophie pulled her cell phone from her jeans pocket, took a photo, and turned it to show her. "You look beautiful."

Mrs. Grabowski smiled when she first saw the picture, but then her eyes got watery. She blinked, and her mouth twitched, and Ava nudged Sophie to put the camera away.

"Sorry," Ava told the old woman's daughter. "We didn't mean to upset her."

"Oh, you didn't upset her. I'm sure she's thinking of old times and perhaps old friends. Right?" She patted her mom's hand.

"Okay." Ava started to leave because she didn't want to see Mrs. Grabowski sad anymore, but Sophie stopped her.

"You know," Sophie said, "we were thinking that your mom might be missing her life back in Ukraine. The staff says she likes that music, so we wondered if she ever used to dance with her family in the old country when she was younger. And if she did, it might be cool if we had a dance for her with costumes and music and stuff, and you could come and any of her other family that's around, and you could dress up, too, and maybe she'd feel like she was there again." Sophie shrugged as if her crazy, elaborate idea were the sort of thing people did in nursing homes all the time.

Mrs. Grabowski's daughter laughed. "We'll have to talk about that next time you come. I see the music is about to start." She nodded toward the folding metal chairs up front, where four kids were settling in, and their teacher was tapping a music stand with her conductor's baton.

"Come on, Soph." Ava tugged Sophie across the room to where the other Andersons were sitting, and they slid into chairs as the orchestra started playing. Grandpa was slouched down in a chair next to Dad, looking as grumpy as ever. *Maybe this pencil-wish project wasn't such a good idea*, Ava thought. Mrs. Grabowski had looked so sad. Maybe she didn't *want* to remember what it was like to be younger and dancing. That had to be hard when you were older and couldn't even walk much or ask for pudding instead of Jell-O.

"You have your saxophone put together already, right?" Sophie whispered when the string quartet started their next number.

"Yeah. It's over by my case, but . . ." Ava swallowed hard. "I don't think I'm going to do it." Because what if she played that song and Grandpa didn't like it at all and he was even grumpier? What if Mrs. Grabowski cried again? What if all the old people hated Ava's song and they started throwing cookies and cups of warm lemonade at her and then Mr. Clemson declared an emergency and flung a chair through the window to get everyone evacuated—all because of Ava and her dumb saxophone? "Maybe another time," Ava whispered.

But when the string quartet finished and the kids started to clear their music stands and chairs, Thomas stood and held up his hands. "Hold on, everyone. Please stay seated. I understand we have one more special musical guest."

Ava looked at Sophie in a panic.

"Sorry," Sophie hissed. "I told him when we first got here so he could give you a good introduction. You *told* me you were playing."

"Put your hands together, people, and let's have a warm Cedar Bay welcome for . . ." Thomas did a fancy music-stand drumroll with his hands. "Miss Ava Anderson!"

18

OPERATION JAZZ

Ava's breath caught in her throat, but she walked over to her saxophone and started fiddling with the strap. Anything was better than sitting there with all these people clapping and waiting for her to do something.

"All set, Ava?" Thomas stood by the empty music stand, waiting for her to put sheet music there and then actually lift the saxophone's mouthpiece to her lips and play it. Which was pretty much impossible, since she couldn't even breathe.

Ava looked back at the folding chairs. Everybody was waiting. Sophie was nodding so enthusiastically she looked like a cartoon character whose head might fall off and roll right across the floor to the cookie table.

Grandpa was looking at her, too. Looking at Ava. Right at her, as if he were actually seeing her. And that didn't happen much anymore.

It made Ava want to play for him. If he could come back from wherever he was most of the time to look at her that way, she could at least try to play him the song.

Ava walked to the front of the room and arranged her sheet music on the stand. She took a deep breath and squeaked out, "This is a song called 'On the Sunny Side of the Street.'" She closed her eyes and breathed in . . . two . . . three . . . four . . . Then out . . . two . . . three . . . four. It calmed her a little.

Without looking back at the audience, Ava lifted the saxophone and started to play.

Scoo-ba-doo-ba-doo-ba-wahhh . . .

The first notes came out shaky, like her voice, but after a few measures, something happened. The sounds were coming from Ava's horn, but she felt as if the music—the feeling of it—had burst out of that Internet video. Cool, not-a-care, chilled-out Johnny Hodges himself. And when she played like that—*Bwahhh-ba-doo-be-doo-wooo*—like she'd never worried about a math test in her life, it felt amazing. It felt sassy and free and fun.

So that's what she did. Ava might have been two feet shorter than Johnny Hodges and a girl, and her skin wasn't quite as dark, but for a few minutes, she felt like him, blasting out the notes. The runs and the *doo-wahs* and the crescendos and the *bip-bip-bops*. She even shook her head a little as she played, just like Johnny Hodges, thinking "Nuh-uh . . . no worries here." Somehow, it felt like her saxophone had captured all that cool and was sending it up through her fingers. She played like that, all the way to the last *Bwahhh-ba-ba-da-ba-doo-wah...wahhh...bwahhhhhhhh.*

Everyone clapped when Ava finished. She looked up, expecting to see her parents smiling her way. But they weren't even looking at her.

They were looking at Grandpa. And Grandpa was pointing right at Ava.

He was *talking.* Shouting! "All right!" He was so loud the Snoozy Gang woke up. "Brava!"

Ava gave a sheepish bow and put her saxophone away. When she went back to sit with her family, her parents both applauded again, and Sophie gave her a big hug.

"Ava, that was *amazing*," Sophie said. Then she looked toward the door, where some people were starting to leave. "I'll be back in a minute, okay?" She tapped the legal pad full of pencil-wish plans. "I want to talk to Mrs. Raymond's family before they go."

Sophie hurried off with the pad, and Ava turned to Grandpa. "What did you think, Grandpa?"

"Spec-tacular!" Grandpa reached for her hand. His was soft and wrinkly and a little cold. Ava tried to remember the last time she'd held Grandpa's hand, way before he went into the nursing home. It had been warmer then, and rougher, probably from working in his garden and building stuff in his garage.

"Spectacular!" Grandpa said again. He laughed and squeezed her hand. "You must be the Rabbit's baby girl!"

"What?" Ava left her hand in his but looked over at her parents. "Who's the Rabbit? Is that some nickname Johnny Hodges had?" Dad shrugged, then smiled and motioned Ava back to her grandfather. "I'm just Ava, Grandpa. But I'm glad you liked the song."

"I *loved* it! It was beautiful." Grandpa had come uncrumpled. He was sitting up, and his eyes were so wide.

He was still nodding to the beat of "On the Sunny Side of the Street," as if the song hadn't stopped playing in his mind.

It gave Ava an idea. "You know, Grandpa, we can put that song on a music player so you can hear it any time."

"Mmm-hmm." Grandpa nodded.

"We'll collect a bunch of songs—Johnny Hodges and—who else do you like? What other jazz did you like to listen to?" she asked him.

"Oh . . ." Grandpa looked out the window as if he were traveling a long, long way in his head. "Duke Ellington. Benny Goodman. Charlie Parker. Cab Calloway . . . mmm, that cat could sing!" Grandpa took a deep breath and started singing. His voice sounded so much younger, even if he wasn't singing anything Ava could understand.

Where was Sophie with the legal pad? They needed to write down those musicians' names before Grandpa went back to slumping in his chair. Ava found Sophie over by the window talking with a woman who turned out to be Mrs. Raymond's daughter-in-law.

"But she *loves* kittens," the woman said, shaking her head as if Sophie had just told her the world was flat.

"I'm sure she does." Sophie smiled. "Just not on her shirts. They had some John Deere tractor sweatshirts where I got this one." Sophie nodded toward Mrs. Raymond, who had put on her new sweatshirt and was smiling down at the monster truck on her stomach.

"Soph, can you help me with something?" Ava pointed toward Grandpa and Sophie looked happy to be ending her no-more-kittens conversation.

"Write down Duke Ellington. I think he's famous; they mentioned him in the online article about Johnny Hodges," Ava said. Sophie scribbled down the name while they walked. "Also Benny Goodman, Charlie Parker, and Cab Calloway." She nodded toward Grandpa, who was still do-wabbity-bipping to his hands, though a little more quietly now.

Sophie sat down beside him. When he finished singing, she said, "Wasn't Ava great?"

"Spec-tacular." Grandpa took a deep breath, then shook his head, closed his eyes, and settled back into his quiet. It was like his new batteries were the Dollar Store kind that only lasted a minute before things slowed down again. But a minute was better than nothing, Ava decided. She turned to Sophie. "Can we put that new music on your iPod tonight?"

Sophie smiled. "Operation Jazz is under way."

19

WORLD-FAMOUS FLAMING DONUTS

The kitchen smelled garlicky when Ava came downstairs Thursday morning. Marcus was printing something off the computer. Emma must have been copying names out of the fridge because her name tag said HELLO MY NAME IS ARUGULA. She was at the table eating toast with marshmallow spread and chocolate chips, which meant Mom had left for work early. Dad was stirring something in a saucepan on the stove. "What are you trying to make?" Ava asked him.

"What do you mean 'trying to make?'" Dad looked hurt.

"Do. Or do not," Marcus called from the printer. "There is no try."

"My teacher says you should try your best even when the math is stupid," Emma-My-Name-Is-Arugula said through a mouthful of toast.

"You should." Marcus sat down next to her at the table and

grabbed an apple from the fruit bowl. "That was just something Yoda said in *Star Wars*." He turned to Dad. "So what are you trying to make?"

"World-famous, super-healthy kale donuts. I got the idea when Mom made that heart attack comment." He opened the oven door and a cloud of earthy-smelling gray-green smoke poured out. "I think the first batch is almost done. Maybe another minute." He went back to the saucepan on the burner. "I'm making garlic frosting to go on top." Dad did a little dance while he stirred.

Marcus laughed, but Ava felt bad for her dad. He was like Sophie sometimes; he got so excited that the reasonable part of his brain just turned off, and then he couldn't see how gross garlic frosting was going to be on any donuts. Kale would just make it green and worse.

Dad started humming, put on an oven mitt, and took out the tray of donuts.

Ava stood up to get a better look. "They don't look quite done." They looked oozy, in fact, and were melting into kale-juice puddles on the hot cookie sheet.

"Donuts have to be deep fried, not baked," Marcus said on his way out the door.

"Maybe they need to bake longer." Ava didn't believe this, but she felt like it might give her dad some hope with his idea, at least until she left for school. "Have you seen Sophie's iPod around?"

Dad put the kale-puddles back in the oven. "Check the counter."

Ava found it. "We filled this up with songs for Grandpa." She put it in the small pocket of her backpack. "More Johnny Hodges and Duke Ellington and—"

"Something smells bad," Emma-My-Name-Is-Arugula said, wrinkling her nose.

"Oh!" Dad ran to the stove, yanked the smoking pot of garlic frosting off the burner, then peeked back into the oven. "Marcus is probably right. I should have fried these." He took them out and stared at the tray for a second. "I know what we can do." He pulled Gram's big olive oil jar from the cupboard, drizzled oil over the kale-puddles, and grabbed the lighter he used when the grill starter didn't work. "This will finish them off. They can be world-famous, half-baked healthy kale donuts!"

Ava knew it would have taken magic to make the kale-puddles fluff up into anything resembling donuts. But she didn't want to hurt Dad's feelings, so she watched while he clicked the lighter and held the flame to the first round, green blob.

The blob caught fire, and before Dad's "Whoa!" was all the way out of his mouth, the entire tray of World-Famous Anderson's General Store Healthy Kale Donuts burst into flames.

"Stop, drop, and roll!" Emma shouted.

"Gimme that oven mitt!" Dad hollered. Ava grabbed it from the counter and threw it to him. He put it on and flipped the whole tray into the sink. By then, all twelve donut infernos were starting to fizzle. Dad stood, panting, watching the smoke rise until the last flame burned itself out. "Open some windows while I go change my clothes," Dad said, "and then I'll drive you guys to school so you're not late."

Ava sighed. If Marcus had been there, he would have said something to prevent this. Something about physics and oils and flammability, and the donuts never would have caught fire. Instead, it had been Ava, thinking not-a-good-idea thoughts but not saying a word. She was opening the kitchen screen door when the fire alarm started screaming. Gram came hurrying into the kitchen in her bathrobe and looked around. "What happened here?"

"World-famous donuts," Ava said.

"They caught on fire," Emma-My-Name-Is-Arugula added.

Gram nodded and opened a window. "That'll get some attention, I suppose." She turned on a fan and started cleaning up the mess.

◅━━━━━━━━▻

As soon as Ava got to school, she realized that it was the day of the adventure course practice in gym class *and* a math quiz. Double doom.

She slipped into her seat while Mr. Farkley marched up and down the rows collecting homework. He stopped by Ava's desk.

"Thank you, Miss Anderson," he said, picking up her paper. "Do you also have your permission slip for the field trip?"

"No. I'm going to bring it tomorrow." Ava had no such plans, but she guessed those were the words that would send

Mr. Farkley and his bushy eyebrows back to his desk. She was right.

"All right then," Mr. Farkley said from up front, "I hope everyone is prepared with a pencil."

Ava was prepared with two. One was a yellow Number Two she'd grabbed from the bottom of her locker. The other was the blue pencil. That one she set carefully on her desk, so it wouldn't roll away. She didn't want to use it. She didn't want to *need* it the way she did, but at the same time, she knew she couldn't take the quiz without knowing it was there if she got stuck.

"You may begin," Mr. Farkley said, and Ava looked at the first question. *Relax. Think,* she told herself. *You can do this. You have the pencil if you need it.*

She picked up the regular yellow pencil. She answered the first question and the second, and worked her way down the page, figuring out problems with parallelograms and right triangles and pi. She looked at the blue pencil a few times but didn't reach for it. Just seeing it there calmed her down, and when she settled in, she found that she really did know most of the answers. There was one she wasn't sure about, but she didn't want to use the pencil, so she guessed.

"Pencils down," Mr. Farkley said, and Ava smiled. She put the yellow one down next to the blue one and let out a long breath. She'd done it. Simply knowing the pencil was there was enough. She'd taken the test without even picking it up.

20

ADVENTURE WAITS FOR NO ONE!

When Ava got to gym class, pretty much everyone had gone outside, and Mr. Avery was waving her out to the field where the course was set up. "Let's go! Today, we're going to practice a few challenges you'll see on the field trip. Come on, Ava! Adventure waits for no one!"

Ava wished Adventure would go on ahead without her, but she followed him outside.

"Choose a station and you can get started." Mr. Avery left her and jogged over to the trees at the side of the clearing where the ropes course was set up. He helped Luke Varnway, Alex Weinstein, and LucyAnn Ward step up onto the low tightrope.

The school's rock-climbing wall was set up at the other end of the field. Mrs. Snell, the other gym teacher, was helping kids get strapped into harnesses to practice, and there were also some low-to-the-ground balance beams set up in the soccer field. Those didn't look too bad, so Ava headed over, stepped up onto one of them, and started teetering her way across.

It was kind of fun, like walking on the curb. Trying this fifty feet above the ground—harness or no harness—would be another story, but Ava didn't mind practicing. She'd figured out that going along with things was the quickest way to be left alone.

If you protest and squeal, people come swooping in to explain to you why you *must* do the scary thing. They promise it will all be okay even though they know no such thing. But if you pretend you have no problem with the scary thing, then nobody bothers you, and on the actual day of the scary thing, you can just not go. Then it's too late for anyone to do anything about it. After you'd thrown up on a couple of field trips, you learned these things.

Ava was counting on it working out that way for the adventure course. No permission slip, no field trip. But she did have to get through the rest of gym class. She looked around, hoping for another easy, no-climbing-involved obstacle to practice, but everything else involved swinging or climbing or other unstable things.

Ava was about to start over on the low balance beam when Sophie came bounding across the field in her new boots.

Ava laughed. "They let you wear those for gym?"

"They have good, solid tread." Sophie lifted her foot to show Ava and then spun around. "Aren't they great? And guess what . . ." She looked around, then leaned in closer to Ava and whispered, "I've decided that today's the day."

"For what?"

Sophie smiled, and her eyes got all big. "I'm going to ask Jason to go out with me!"

"You are?" Thinking about what Sophie was about to do made Ava's stomach all twisty. "Why now?"

"Why not?" Sophie did a cartwheel. "That way, we'll be able to sit together on the bus for the field trip. He's probably been wanting to ask me for a while but he's too nervous or something, you know?"

Ava nodded. She understood nervous.

"I've got it all planned out," Sophie went on. "Look over there." She pointed quickly to the rock wall. Ava turned and caught a glimpse of Jason before Sophie hissed. "Stop staring! He's going to know I'm talking about him!"

"Sorry. But . . . you're just going to walk up to him and ask him out? Just like that?"

She laughed. "I already know what he'll say, right?"

Ava stole another glance at the amazing Jason. "Who's that with him?"

"Jessica Bainbridge, maybe?" Sophie squinted, then waved her hand. "It doesn't matter." And she ran across the soccer field toward the rock wall.

The closer Sophie got, the more Ava wanted to call her back. Because Jason wasn't just talking to Jessica Bainbridge. He was hanging on her. And she was laughing and twisting her hair and touching his arm and looking a whole lot like his girlfriend.

Sophie walked right up to them, stepped in front of Jessica, and tossed her hair.

No, no, no, Ava thought. She tried sending Sophie thought waves across the soccer field. *Danger! Danger! Step away from the boy.*

But all Ava could do was watch the whole thing play out like a silent movie.

She saw Sophie lean forward, smiling. She saw Jason take a step back and shake his head. She saw Jessica cross her arms, then get right up in Sophie's face and start waving her hands. She saw Sophie step back, then turn and walk away, then run. She ran right past Ava into school, tears streaking down her cheeks.

Ava looked for Sophie in the girls' bathroom but couldn't find her. She didn't need to find her to know what had happened. The pencil had been wrong about Jason.

Sophie showed up halfway through science with a pass from guidance. She was blotchy-faced but not crying anymore. She waited until Mrs. Ruppert was turned to the SMART Board and then slipped Ava a note.

Do you have the pencil?

Ava did. But she was a little afraid of what Sophie might do with it. Was she angry enough to break it in half or throw it out? Ava couldn't very well lie to Sophie, though, so she nodded.

Sophie wrote:

Ask it what the heck happened!

Ava looked up from the note. Mrs. Ruppert was tapping her SMART Board but couldn't get her video to play. She went to call the tech guy, and everybody started talking.

Ava took out the pencil and wrote:

Why doesn't Jason want to go out with Sophie?

"Because he's going out with Jessica Bainbridge," the voice said.

"What did it say?" Sophie whispered as the tech guy climbed up on a chair to adjust some wires.

"It says he's going out with Jessica Bainbridge."

"Then why did it say he liked me?" Sophie hissed.

"I . . . I don't know." Ava swallowed hard. Sophie sounded mad, like this was Ava's fault. "Maybe it messes up sometimes."

"You didn't tell me that. I never would have done that if the stupid pencil hadn't—"

"Okay, everyone, it's fixed," Mrs. Ruppert said. "Let's get back to work."

Sophie gave a sharp sigh and turned away.

Ava found her worksheet and started filling in responses, but out of the corner of her eye, she saw Jessica Bainbridge's friend Mikayla toss a note onto Sophie's desk.

Sophie blinked at it, then unfolded it and sucked in her breath. Ava only had to lean over a little to read it:

STAY AWAY FROM OTHER PEOPLE'S BOYFRIENDS

Sophie's eyes filled with tears, and Ava understood why. Sophie should have known. It was obvious to every other person within a mile of the rock wall that Jessica and Jason were going out. But instead of believing her own eyes, Sophie had believed the pencil.

Sophie crumpled the note and shoved it deep in her pocket. When the bell rang, she shot out of her seat. Ava figured she'd be waiting in the hall so they could walk home together.

But she wasn't.

21

ANSWERS AND LIES

Ava walked home alone. She and Sophie had planned to go to the nursing home together to drop off the iPod with Grandpa's songs. Ava didn't want to go by herself, but she thought that was a crummy reason for him not to have music, so halfway home, she changed her mind and took a detour to Cedar Bay. The November wind was getting colder, and Ava's hands were freezing by the time she pulled open the door.

When Ava headed toward the community room, Thomas stopped her. "Hey, Miss Ava! It's not Wednesday. What brings you here?"

Ava pulled out the iPod and headphones. "I wanted Grandpa to have this. We put music on it, like that song he loved last night."

Thomas looked over his shoulder, down the long hallway. "Your grandpa's asleep right now. He's had a bit of a tough day. But I'll give this to him as soon as he wakes up, all right?"

"Okay. Thanks." Ava left and headed for home. It really wasn't okay. She'd wanted to stay and see if Grandpa liked the music. She'd wanted to do that with Sophie, to put headphones on Grandpa and play songs and see his face wake up like it did when she'd played Johnny Hodges. But Sophie was mad at her and Grandpa wasn't even awake and everything was ruined.

What if Sophie stayed mad forever? Ava shivered and zipped up her jacket. She couldn't imagine school without Sophie. Or weekends without Sophie. Without Sophie, Ava would never do anything brave. She'd probably never even have another friend because it was always Sophie who introduced her to people and made her feel okay about being someplace other than her bedroom eating Gram's cookies and reading books.

Lucy and Ethel were out when Ava got home. Ethel lowered her head and started toward her, so Ava veered off into the grass. The mud sucked at her sneakers, and she felt cold wetness seeping through her sock. Nobody would be impressed with her fancy green ladder-laces now.

Ava's eyes burned with tears as she trudged up to the house. Why was Sophie mad at her? Ava wasn't the one who'd told Sophie to start asking the pencil about boys and crushes and like-liking people. Ava wasn't the one who'd brought up Jason Marzigliano. She hadn't even known who he was until the pencil mentioned him.

Ava took a deep breath. Maybe Sophie was upset but not mad. Sometimes, Ava couldn't tell the difference. She just assumed that whenever anybody wasn't happy, it was her fault.

When Ava opened the kitchen door, there were cookies on

the counter, along with a note that said Gram was taking a nap. Gram never used to take so many naps. What if she was sick like Grandpa and had to go live at Cedar Bay, too?

Ava's stomach gave an awful twist. Even Gram's warm cookies didn't look good.

Ava tried taking her deep counting breaths, but they came out all uneven and shaky and made her wonder if there was something wrong with her, too. Maybe she had one of those respiratory diseases people got on that epidemic episode of *Boston Med*. What if Ava had that disease? If she got sicker and sicker and died, Sophie probably wouldn't even go to her funeral.

Enough with the what-ifs, Ava thought. But she couldn't make herself stop. She had to fix this. Sophie had to talk to her.

Ava pulled off her stupid-goat-muddy sneakers, headed for the computer, and typed a message to Sophie.

Hey—want to come over? Gram made cookies.

She sent it and stared, waiting and hoping for a fast reply. If everything was okay, Sophie would say yes. Whatever had gone wrong in somebody's day, Gram's cookies made things better, and Sophie totally knew that. Her answer came right away.

Can't. Running errands with Mom.

K, Ava typed, and logged out. But she sat staring at the screen. Normally, Sophie would have invited Ava to come along or at least told her what the errands were. Ava wondered if there even were errands. She'd ask the pencil, the way she'd asked it how Maya and Lucy felt about her. She was probably worried over nothing. The pencil would probably tell her everything was fine.

Ava went to her room, took out the pencil, and wrote:

Does Sophie really have to run errands with her mom right now?

"No," the voice said. As if that should have been obvious. Ava wrote:

Why did Sophie lie to me?

"Because she's angry about what happened with Jason Marzigliano," the pencil answered.

That wasn't my fault. It was your fault, Ava wrote.

The pencil didn't say anything.

"Ava! I didn't hear you come home," Gram said from the doorway.

Ava put the pencil down and turned to face her. "I saw your nap note, so I was quiet. I haven't been home long."

Gram came in and kissed her on the head, then stepped back to look at her. "Are you having a tough day? You're blinking a lot."

Ava tried not to blink. Her eyes burned. "I'm okay."

Gram squinted at her. "You sure?" Ava nodded, but she knew she was going to be on the list in the Jesus notebook tonight, along with the yahoo running Mom's country and the people of war-torn Sudan. That was fine. Ava would take all the prayers she could get.

"How come you were taking a nap?"

"Eh . . ." Gram shrugged. "My stomach's a little off this afternoon."

"Again?" It seemed like Gram's stomach was never "on" any-more. "Did you go to the doctor?"

"Oh, no. I'm fine." Gram waved at the air. "I'm going to start dinner." She headed for the stairs.

Ava picked up the pencil.

Is something wrong with Gram?

"Yes," the voice said. It didn't elaborate. Ava wanted to throw the pencil across the room or break it in half, but she couldn't. She needed it.

Her hands were shaking when she wrote the next question:

Is Gram going to die?

"Yes," the voice answered, as calmly as if it were telling her the sky was blue. Ava put the pencil down and pressed the heels of her palms into her eyes. No, no, no! Gram couldn't die; she couldn't leave Ava and Mom and Dad and Marcus and Emma. They all needed her so much. No!

Ava had to call her parents. Maybe Gram was only going to die if whatever it was got worse. Could a pencil-fact change once the pencil said it was true? Jason Marzigliano sure changed. Maybe the pencil would be wrong again. Maybe if they got Gram to a doctor right away, right now, she wouldn't die. Ava had to call her parents. She had to tell Gram. But what would she say? Gram obviously had no idea how sick she was. She was going to be terrified. Or worse, she wouldn't even believe Ava and she'd just laugh it all off and then head down to the kitchen to make dinner and probably collapse right there.

Ava couldn't slow her breathing. She felt like she might throw up or pass out or maybe both, but she forced herself to slow down. She took a shuddery breath and reached for the pencil. She needed to know how soon it was going to happen. In shaky letters, she wrote:

When is Gram going to die?

The pencil didn't answer. Ava hated it. She choked out a sob and wrote so hard the tip broke off the pencil but she kept going with the blunt point:

Why won't you answer my question? Why won't you tell me when Gram is going to die?

"Because," the pencil said. "I do not predict the future."

Ava thought her head might explode.

Then why did you tell me she's going to die??

"She is," the voice answered calmly. "So are you. Everyone is going to die eventually."

Ava dropped the pencil, sank back in her chair, and stared at the ceiling. She felt like a balloon that somebody blew too full of air and then let go of so it raced all around the room and ended up a deflated, wrinkled blob.

She couldn't make her heart slow down. She took a deep, shaky breath.

Gram isn't going to die any time soon, she told herself.

Then why was she feeling so rotten all the time?

Ava took a few more deep breaths. That dumb pencil was going to tell her what she wanted to know, whether it wanted to or not. She thought about how to say it, then wrote:

What is the official medical explanation for why Gram has been feeling sick to her stomach lately?

"Lactose intolerance," the voice said decisively. Ava scribbled down the words, then wrote:

What does that mean?

Ava realized as soon as she wrote it that she'd just broken the don't-ask-questions-Google-can-answer rule.

"Lactose intolerance," the voice said, "means that the body cannot easily digest lactose, a type of natural sugar found in milk and dairy products."

Ava stared at the words. Lactose intolerance. Gram wasn't going to die. She wasn't even sick. Not really. She just had to stop drinking milk. That was all.

Ava felt as if her whole life had been stolen away and then given back to her, only brighter and shinier than before. She could go downstairs now and look up lactose intolerance on the computer and then show Gram. She'd say they talked about it in life science or something and then Gram could go to the doctor and have him tell her for sure and then everything would be back to normal. She stood up and started for the door, then paused and looked at the pencil on the desk.

She was pretty sure the pencil wouldn't respond, but she picked it up and wrote:

Thank you.

Just in case it could hear.

DANCING RED SHOES

Gram was in the kitchen stirring Alfredo sauce when Ava came downstairs. Perfect. "Okay if I use the computer to look up something we talked about in science class?" She had it all planned out.

"Sure." Gram nodded and raised a spoonful of steaming cheese sauce from the pot. She blew on it and opened her mouth just as Ava realized, *Dairy product!*

"Gram, don't eat that!"

Gram jumped. She dropped the spoon into the pot on the stove. "Good gracious, Ava, you almost gave me a heart attack." Gram pulled some tongs from the drawer and fished out the spoon. "What on earth is the problem?"

"It's just . . ." Shoot. She hadn't even had a chance to pull up the website, so now her warning was all kinds of suspicious. "Hold on a second and I'll show you." She did a quick search and found a site about lactose intolerance. "Look at this." She turned the computer monitor toward Gram. "In science today, we were studying . . . umm . . ." She skimmed the page for a science-class word. "Enzymes. And then we talked about lactose intolerance and it made me think about you because you have some of these symptoms, right?"

Gram put the cheesy spoon in the sink and came over to look. "Well, I'll be . . ." She read the page, nodding slowly, then raised her thin eyebrows. "Sounds like you might be onto something, Dr. Ava. I'll lay off the cheese tonight and see how I feel later on."

"Good idea." Ava read the rest of the page and started worrying again. It said lactose intolerance was sometimes linked to other diseases like cystic fibrosis, which sounded bad. What if Gram had that? Plus some people with lactose intolerance had trouble getting enough calcium and then they broke bones and stuff. "Gram, this says even if you're pretty sure you have this, you should go to the doctor to make sure nothing else is wrong."

"Makes sense," Gram said, pulling the salad out of the fridge.

"What are you talking to the doctor about?" Dad breezed into the kitchen with a new poster under his arm.

"Ava has diagnosed my stomach troubles as lactose intolerance." Gram sighed at the pot of Alfredo sauce. "No more cheese for me for a while." She nodded to Dad's poster. "What's the latest?"

Dad turned it around so they could see.

ANDERSON'S GENERAL STORE: HOME OF THE WORLD-FAMOUS PYRAMID ICE CREAM CONE

"It'll be like that world-famous square ice cream cone in Idaho. Only pointier."

Ava was happy to have something to talk about besides Gram being sick. "How are you going to make it a pyramid?" Dad served up plenty of ice cream cones in the summer, but they were all messy-shaped lumps.

"I'm not sure yet." Dad rolled up the poster and snapped a rubber band around it. "But I think this may be the one."

Mom got home with Marcus and Emma-My-Name-Is-Honda then. Mom was stressed because she'd had to leave her office early to pick Emma up from soccer. Marcus was grumpy because Riley Sutton cheated at chess club—"He took his hand off the piece and then moved it again. You can't *do* that."

And Emma was furious that her new coach refused to allow self-assigned names. "He said Honda's a car, not a girl. And I said why can't it be both, but then he just said no. And there are three Emmas," she whined, "so I have to be Emma A."

"There are worse things to be," Gram said, picking at her salad. She still looked tired to Ava. So after the dinner dishes were washed and dried, Ava went back to her room and picked up the pencil to check on that other disease the website had talked about:

Does Gram have cystic fibrosis?

"No," the voice said.

Good. One bad thing down. But what if there was something else wrong?

Does Gram have cancer?

"No."

Does Gram have heart problems?

"No."

"Ava?" Mom's voice made her jump.

Her mom laughed. "Sorry to startle you. You left this in the front hallway, and I figured you'd want to practice." She set Ava's saxophone by the desk.

Ava slid her math homework over the pencil questions before her mom had a chance to see. "I'll practice later. I've got homework."

Mom nodded and headed for the door. "Get started. I don't want you up too late."

She closed the door behind her, and Ava pushed the math paper aside. She looked down at the list of questions and felt her chest tighten. What if there was something else wrong with Gram—something awful—and she hadn't asked the right question? Or what if there was something wrong with Mom or Dad? What if there was something wrong with *her* and she just didn't know it yet? What if it was one of those awful diseases from *Boston Med*?

Ava looked at the pencil. There wasn't going to be enough lead in the world to ask everything she needed to know to be okay.

The blue pencil was starting to remind Ava of the red shoes in a fairy tale Gram told her once. There was this little girl who was poor and had almost nothing except a pair of tattered red shoes that she'd made for herself, and she loved them. One day, a wealthy woman took her in and ran a warm bath for her and gave her new clothes. When the girl came out of the bath, all clean, she asked for her shoes, but the woman had thrown them away. She took the girl to the shoemaker to have new black shoes made for church, but the girl saw these shiny bright-red shoes on the shelf and asked for those instead. The old woman's vision was so bad she didn't notice, and the shoemaker winked at the girl and gave her the shoes she wanted.

Ava remembered thinking that was pretty great. But the next part of the story was awful. The girl put on her red shoes and went to church, and you weren't supposed to wear red shoes to church back then for some reason, and everyone stared. And somehow, when she left church, she started dancing. At first it was fine, but then she started dancing faster and faster and couldn't stop, and someone had to run and catch her and carry her home. The old woman put the shoes up on a shelf and told her never to wear them again.

That would have been enough for Ava, but this girl couldn't stop staring at the shoes and longing for them, and one day she put them back on and it was even worse. She danced faster and longer than ever, until she was exhausted and crying, but she couldn't stop, and finally, she went to the town executioner and begged him to cut the straps of the shoes to get them off her feet. He tried that, but it didn't work. And finally—this part made Ava shiver—she begged him to cut off her feet. He did, and the shoes just kept on dancing with her awful bleeding feet inside.

"That's one of the original fairy tales," Gram had said, pulling Ava close to her on the couch. "Before they cleaned them all up in the interest of not scarring children for life."

At the time, Ava had loved hearing the secret, scary fairy tale. But her worries were bigger now. Sometimes, it felt like the "what-ifs" in her head might dance her over a cliff one day, too.

Ava looked down at the pencil.

She picked it up.

She couldn't *not* pick it up.

Do I have cancer?

"No," the pencil answered right away.

Does Dad have cancer?

"No."

Does Mom have cancer?

Ava was already poised to scribble the next question when the pencil answered, just as quick and calm as always.

"Yes."

23

THE APPOINTMENT

"You know, your jeans would last longer if you didn't throw them in the wash every other day."

Ava jumped about a mile, but Mom didn't even notice. She'd walked right back through Ava's open door and was piling folded laundry onto the closet shelves. When Mom turned around, Ava couldn't stop staring.

Where was it? Where was the cancer? In her brain? In her lungs like their neighbor Mrs. Groves who died last year? But Mrs. Groves was a smoker. Mom didn't do that. Could she still have lung cancer?

Mom dropped a pile of socks on Ava's dresser, then held out a piece of paper. "Here's your permission slip for the field trip on Monday."

At first, Ava just stared at that, too. Her mom shook the paper. Ava took it and looked down at the cheerful signature sending her to her doom. "Where'd you get this?" She'd been so careful not to leave it around.

"Mr. Avery emailed it to me. He thought you might have misplaced yours." Mom gave her a pointed look. "You know how we feel about these things, Ava. All you need to do is try. I know you're nervous, so I told Mr. Avery I'd come along to chaperone. I think it sounds like fun anyway. If it's awful, you can sit out the more difficult courses and read, okay? I promise."

Ava stared at her mom again. Mom couldn't go on that field trip. She couldn't be climbing around in the trees. She was sick. Only she didn't even know it. Ava's eyes drifted from the top of her mother's head down her tall, lean body. She looked so healthy.

Maybe the pencil was wrong. It was wrong about Jason liking Sophie. *Oh, please, please, please let it be wrong about this,* Ava thought.

"Why are you looking at me like that?"

"Sorry . . . I was just thinking. I must have zoned out." Ava shrugged. She tried to look at her mom's face, tried to keep from scanning her body as if she could make the cancer light up and show itself.

"Do you feel okay?" Ava blurted.

"Yes." Mom frowned. "Why? What's wrong? Are you really this worked up over a field trip?"

Ava shook her head. She needed to know if Mom felt anything unusual. But she couldn't ask that. "I asked how you feel because you look tired."

"I'd be less tired if you and Marcus would wear your clothes more than ten minutes before you put them in the wash."

"Sorry," Ava said. "Thanks for the permission slip."

"Yeah . . . I know you really mean that." Mom laughed and squatted down next to her at the desk. "Remember . . . you are not only really smart and super-kind, and . . . fast? Something like that. Anyway, you're a pretty brave bunny, too."

Ava felt a lump in her throat. That quote—or something like it—was from an Easter book she and Mom used to read, *The Country Bunny and the Little Gold Shoes*. Easter was five months away. Would Mom even be here then? The lump in Ava's throat swelled up, and tears spilled out of her eyes.

"Oh, honey . . ." Mom wrapped her in a hug. "I can tell you're having a tough day. But everything's going to be fine."

No, it wasn't. But Mom didn't know why. And Ava couldn't tell her. All she could do was cry.

Finally, Ava got her sobs under control, and Mom gave her one more squeeze before she stood up. "You are going to be fine. And I mean it . . . I'll be there for you on the field trip. Okay?"

Ava nodded. She knew she'd start crying again if she tried to talk.

Mom started to leave. Ava held onto the armrests of her chair. She wanted to jump up and tackle Mom and have Dad rush her to the hospital. But what would she say? *My pencil says you're sick?*

Mom pulled the door closed behind her, and Ava turned

back to the pencil. She needed to think. She needed more information.

Ava took a deep breath. Her hand trembled as she wrote, *What kind of cancer does my mom have?*

"Breast cancer," the voice said.

Ava wanted to throw up. She had to tell Mom about the pencil so she'd go to the hospital and get help. But what if Mom didn't believe it? What if she wouldn't even try the pencil for herself? Ava looked down at the thing; it didn't look even a little bit believable. It was a weird too-bright blue color and now it was getting stubby from all that sharpening, too.

What Ava needed was for Mom to go to the doctor and find out on her own. That was how people were supposed to find out they were sick. There must be some test they could do for breast cancer. Ava didn't have to tell Mom about the pencil or the cancer; she just had to get her to see a doctor. Mom believed doctors. She'd do what they said and then she could get better without the pencil getting involved at all. If it was the kind of cancer that they could treat. On *Boston Med*, most of it wasn't and people lost their hair with all that treatment and then died anyway and everybody cried.

Ava's eyes burned with tears. *No. No. No.* She swiped them with her sleeve and grabbed the pencil.

Is my mom's cancer the kind that kills people really fast no matter what?

The pencil didn't answer. How could it ignore her questions

at a time like this? It would probably tell her that stupid cancer has free will, too.

Ava stood up and swallowed hard. The lump in her throat didn't go away, but she took a deep breath and went down to the kitchen.

"Mom?"

"What's up?" Mom was scrubbing a brownie pan in the sink as if everything was just fine. As if she didn't have cancer somewhere eating away at her.

"Have you been to the doctor lately?"

"Not in a while." Mom put the brownie pan upside down on the counter and tossed Ava a dish towel. "How come?" She started loading silverware into the dishwasher.

Ava picked up the pan and started drying. "Just wondering. We were talking in health class about how when you get older, you should go for checkups more often." There was a fleck of burned brownie stuck in one corner of the pan. Ava scraped at it with her fingernail and tried to make her voice sound casual, but her heart was pounding in her chest. "Like to get screened for cancer and stuff. Do you do that?"

"Well, sure."

"How often?"

"Once a year."

"Is this year's coming up soon?" Ava blurted.

"Actually, I think it's next week." Mom started to look up at the calendar over the sink, but then she turned and looked at

Ava. "Why are you asking me this? Have you been watching *Boston Med* again?"

"No. I told you, we were talking about it in school." Ava turned, grateful to have the brownie pan to put away so she could hide her watery eyes. "And they told us to remind our parents. It's homework." There. That ought to do it.

"Well, far be it from me to blow off your homework." Mom squinted at the calendar, then frowned. "Huh. I actually have my annual mammogram scheduled for Monday. I'll need to switch that. It's the same day as your field trip."

"Don't do that. You should go to your appointment. I'm sure they have plenty of other—"

"Ava." Mom folded her arms. "You are not getting out of the field trip."

"I'll go on the field trip by myself!" Ava blurted. She thought fast. "I'm just . . . tired today. I *was* nervous, but I did the balance beams in gym for practice and I think it's going to be fun. But I want to do it on my own." She did her best to look brave and independent. "I want to prove to myself I can do it, and if you're there chaperoning . . ." Ava shrugged.

"Really?" Mom looked at her.

Ava made a decision. If risking her life swinging around the trees on a bunch of flimsy cables was the only way to get her mom to the doctor, that was that. She'd go on the stupid trip so Mom would go to the doctor. "Really." Ava nodded. "I'm sure they have enough chaperones anyway. They always sign up extras."

Mom smiled at Ava. "All right, then. You go off to the adventure course, and I'll go to my appointment and you can tell your health teacher we all did our homework."

"Oh, thank you!" Ava forgot to sound casual. "I mean, that's exactly what you're supposed to do. I think they're hoping the parents who don't take care of that stuff will get reminded when kids ask."

Mom nodded. "Not a bad idea, actually." She closed the dishwasher and tipped her head to look at Ava again. "You know, I'm really proud of you, working through your anxiety like this."

Ava nodded. "I was kind of stressed earlier. But I'm fine now," she said. Then she added in her head, *I will be, anyway. As soon as I know you're all right.*

24

CHICKEN POOP BINGO

All weekend, Ava tried not to use the pencil. She spent Saturday helping Dad clear out the vegetable garden, now that it was below freezing at night and nothing was growing anymore.

Dad tugged on a fat stalk of overgrown broccoli. "How about world-famous oatmeal cookies?"

"What would make them world famous?" Marcus asked, kicking at a pile of weeds.

"Well, they could be truly excellent cookies." The broccoli let go, and Dad flew back a few steps but caught his balance. "Or we could include some off-the-wall ingredient. The G and R Tavern has a world-famous fried bologna sandwich with cheese, pickles, and onions."

"Eww. Where's that?" Emma-My-Name-Is-Toyota squealed.

"Waldo, Ohio."

"Where's Waldo?" Marcus said, and he and Ava both cracked up.

Dad was so focused on the world-famous bologna he didn't even get the joke. "Ohio. I told you that. So maybe we could do a twist on the ingredients. Oatmeal and . . ." He pulled out a withered pepper plant and sniffed it. "Jalapeños!"

"Dad, maybe cooking isn't your thing," Marcus said. "What if you tried to have . . . I don't know . . . a world-famous *event*? When you had me looking for ideas, I found a wiener dog race in Texas. And this place in Belize has chicken poop bingo, where—"

Emma burst out laughing. "Chicken poop bingo! Hahaha!" Then she started singing, "I had a chicken, yes I did, played bingo with her poop, oh, B . . . I . . . N-G-O, B . . . I . . . N-G-O . . ."

Marcus threw a clod of roots and dirt at her. "It's a real thing," he said. "They make the chicken coop into this grid, and then people buy squares for ten dollars each. Wherever the bird poops, the person with that square wins the money."

"Hmm. We don't have chickens, but some kind of event might be good," Dad said. "Maybe we could have a wheelbarrow race." He started running across the lawn with the wheelbarrow while weeds spilled over the sides.

Emma giggled and chased after him. "World-famous wheelbarrow!"

Ava wished she could run around with a wheelbarrow and laugh, too. But her pencil-news felt like all she could carry today. She sighed.

It must have been a loud sigh because Marcus turned to her. "What's wrong with you?"

Ava shrugged and started stacking the empty tomato cages. "I'm worried."

She waited for Marcus to ask why, but he just nodded. "Dad says Grandpa's still mostly staying in bed."

That made her look up. "How come?"

"I don't know. You know he's been sick this week, right?"

Ava nodded, even though she hadn't known. Why hadn't Mom told her?

"Dad said they're doing tests on his heart." Marcus shrugged. "He's just old, I guess."

"Yeah." Ava pulled out a dead tomato plant. There was a roly-poly bug underneath, looking all surprised to see light. "Hey, Marcus . . . do you feel like it's weird how Grandpa is Mom's dad, but it's always Dad who's talking about him and making us all go to family night and stuff?"

"No." Marcus answered, his voice certain as the pencil's.

Ava poked the roly-poly bug, and it curled up tight.

"He and Mom have barely spoken since Grandma died," Marcus went on, "and Grandpa had that gambling thing and lost our college money."

"What?" For a second, it almost made Ava forget about Mom's cancer.

Marcus tipped his head and looked at her. "I didn't realize you didn't know. Mom and Dad were talking about it while we were cleaning out Grandpa's apartment over the summer. You were at Sophie's. They either didn't know I was in the living room packing up books or didn't care. But yeah . . ."

"What happened?"

"When Grandma Marion died, Grandpa went kind of wild. He flew to Las Vegas and played slot machines or blackjack or something—won a boatload of money for a while, too, then— bam! He went to some casino in Atlantic City and lost everything." Marcus brushed some dirt off his knee. "Grandma had told Mom that money she left with him would be for our college." He shrugged. "But that's not gonna happen."

"Wow." Ava looked at Marcus. "Wow," she said again, this time because she suddenly understood why he'd gotten so serious about physics and his science projects, why he was so intense. He was hoping for a scholarship. He *had* to hope for a scholarship now. And Mom . . . Mom was the most money-careful person Ava knew. No wonder she was furious. "Wow."

"You want to shoot baskets?" Marcus asked.

"No thanks." Ava hesitated. He'd told her a secret; it felt like she should tell him about Mom. But she couldn't. He'd find out soon. She swallowed hard and went inside.

Ava tried to read her book for English, but her head was spinning like one of those slot machine screens, with thoughts popping up and then whirring away again. Grandpa's gambling. College. Marcus. The general store. Mom. Mom's cancer. Even thinking that word made Ava shiver. She couldn't imagine what it would be like when Mom came home from that appointment and said it aloud. *Cancer.*

Ava took a shaky breath. She needed Sophie back so much. She tried to message her again but only got a quick: SORRY CAN'T TALK. OUT HIKING WITH DAD AND JENNA. Ava guessed that was a lie without even asking the pencil.

25

SAD SONGS

On Sunday morning, Ava finished her homework. She tried to fill up the afternoon with saxophone practice. Over and over she played the songs Miss Romero had given her. She was getting all the notes to the *Titanic* song, but it didn't sound right. It didn't sound true. Ava wondered if watching that sad scene in the movie would help, but she decided she was too full of her own sadness to make room for any of Leonardo DiCaprio's, so she put that piece away and took out the Johnny Hodges song she'd played for Grandpa.

That one was better. After she played it a few times, her stomach felt less twisty. It wasn't going to help her with the audition, though. She had to play one of the pieces she'd been given, and the more Ava thought about it, she couldn't imagine surviving Monday. She had to go to school and get on a bus bound for the Adventure Course of Doom, and if she survived that, she'd have jazz tryouts after school.

Ava put her saxophone away and sat down at her desk.

The pencil was there. She'd been trying so hard not to use it, but there it was. So she picked it up.

Ava had tried all day to keep the questions about Mom penned up in the back of her mind. Now, they spilled out, one after another.

What time is Mom's appointment on Monday?

"One o'clock."

Is her doctor good at treating cancer?

No answer.

What is her doctor's success rate with breast cancer patients?

"Dr. Vakara's five-year survival rate for breast cancer patients is sixty-one percent."

Ava almost choked on the lump that welled up in her throat. That was awful! Sixty-one percent was hardly more than half.

Does that mean my mom has almost a 50 percent chance of dying?

"No."

Why not?

"Because her particular type of breast cancer responds better to treatment than many others."

That answer should have made Ava feel better, but it didn't. Which others? What kind of cancer was it? And what was it doing in there, invisible in her mom's body? Had it already started to spread? Ava knew the pencil wasn't always right. It had totally messed up on Jason and Sophie. But what if the pencil *had* been right about the cancer but wrong about this particular detail and really, Mom's cancer was way worse?

Ava's hand couldn't keep up with her frantic thoughts. It was like that *I Love Lucy* episode Dad showed her and Sophie once, where these chocolates kept flying down an assembly line and Lucy and Ethel couldn't keep up so they tried to eat them all and ended up a mess. Probably sick, too. That's how Ava felt. But she couldn't stop.

What kind of breast cancer does Mom have?

"Stage one B."

What does that mean?

The pencil was quiet.

Ava's eyes burned with tears. How was that not specific enough? She needed to know what stage one B meant, and she couldn't go downstairs and google it or everybody would want to know why. Her fist tightened around the pencil. She hated it so much. But she needed it.

Her hand shook as she wrote, What are the characteristics of stage 1B breast cancer?

"With stage one B breast cancer," the voice said, "the tumor is two centimeters in diameter or smaller, and there is evidence that cancer has spread to the lymph nodes with small clusters of cells no larger than a grain of rice."

Lymph nodes. They hadn't learned that in life science yet, but it sounded bad.

What are lymph n—

Ava hurled the pencil and its stupid broken tip right across the room. It bounced off the door with a *crack*, and Ava put her head down on her desk and sobbed. She cried until her throat hurt and her head pounded and her eyes were all puffy and she got the hiccups.

She finally quieted enough to hear a knock on the door.

She didn't bother trying to sound okay. She wasn't. "Yeah?"

The door opened slowly, and Gram peered in. "Honey, what's wrong?

Tears spilled down Ava's face again. She couldn't claim nothing was wrong. This was more obvious than blinking. "My pencil broke."

It sounded stupid, but Gram was the kind of person who knew she didn't need to point that out. "I see." She looked thoughtfully at the blue pencil on the floor, picked it up, walked over to the pencil sharpener on the wall, and started turning the handle, grinding away at it.

Ava could see it getting shorter, being eaten before her eyes. "Gram, I can do that!"

"That's okay. It's done." She held the stubby pencil up as if it were a rose and presented it to Ava at her desk. "Here you are."

"Thanks." Ava took a shaky breath.

"Ava?" Gram stood waiting.

"Yeah?"

"This is not about your pencil, is it?"

Ava shook her head.

"Want to talk about it?"

She did. So much. But she couldn't. "No, I'll be okay."

Gram nodded. "If you change your mind, I'll be in the

family room watching CNN. Been a busy day out there in the world."

"Who are you praying for?" Ava asked.

"The president—don't tell your mom because she can't stand him—the people who've had to leave home in that civil war in Africa, that singer you like . . . what's her name?"

"Katina D? What's wrong with her?"

"I saw that music video where she's out in the wind and rain wearing practically nothing. She's going to catch pneumonia." Gram shook her head. "So I'm praying somebody finds her some pants and a coat. Let's see . . . there's also that Olympic skier who broke her leg training, all the workers who are unemployed . . ." Gram ticked off the list on her fingers. ". . . and you." She kissed the top of Ava's head and started for the door.

"Gram?" Ava took a shaky breath. "Maybe you should pray for people with cancer. I saw something about that on the news today, too."

Gram nodded. "Consider it done."

26

THE FIELD TRIP OF DOOM

Bright sunshine lit up Monday morning. The blue sky was like a giant billboard that read PERFECT DAY FOR THE FIELD TRIP OF DOOM!

For a moment, when she first woke, Ava had thought about being sick. When she was anxious, the journey from nervous-queasy stomach to actual vomiting was a short one. She was already halfway there, and if she threw up, she'd have to stay home.

But then Mom would cancel her appointment. That couldn't happen.

Mom had to go to the doctor. Which meant Ava had to go on the field trip.

So she left for school early and didn't wait for Sophie. Ava dropped her saxophone off in the band room, turned her permission slip in at the office, and headed to the cafeteria where

Mr. Avery was taking attendance. When he finished calling names, he said, "Okay, you can head out to the bus now."

Ava didn't bother looking for Sophie. Sophie was probably still mad, and Ava knew she had to do this on her own anyway. She marched out the cafeteria door, eyes straight ahead like a soldier marching into battle. She had a plan.

Ava had read online that the adventure course had a policy— if you fell off a course and ended up dangling by your harness and couldn't get yourself back up, they'd send somebody to rescue you. And once you got rescued, you were done for the day. You couldn't go back up there and keep trying. Ava figured that was to make sure people tried really hard to rescue themselves before they called for help. But it didn't matter why the course had that policy. All that mattered was that you were done for the day if you got stuck and got rescued. Nobody could bully you into trying again because you weren't allowed anyway.

Ava didn't give Sophie a chance to not sit with her on the bus. Ava took the first open seat—next to Amy Titherington—who was already playing some game on her phone and didn't even look up. Perfect. Ava pulled out her book. She just wanted to get there and go through the training so she could fail and get rescued and be done.

When the bus pulled into the adventure course parking lot an hour later, Ava got off without looking back. She hurried into the lobby with Mr. Avery and collected her harness. The girls working behind the counter seemed more concerned about Tom, the cute new guide from the community college, than they were about Ava's survival. "Go on out and they'll give you directions for setting up your harness," one girl said with a wave, then turned back to her friend. "Anyway, Amber told me Tom had a girlfriend but they broke up. How could anyone break up with those dimples?"

Ava went out to the porch and sat down near Luke Varnway at one of the picnic tables. Leo walked by and quacked at him. Luke got up and followed Leo, stepping all over the back of his sneakers the whole way. Leo quacked louder. And every quack reminded Ava of all the messes she'd made with her dumb magic pencil. She couldn't give Luke his secret back. She couldn't undo what the pencil said about her mom. She couldn't make it not true, and now that she knew, she couldn't *un*know it.

Ava looked at her watch. It was 9:08. Her mom would be leaving for the doctor's office in a few hours. Not long after that, she'd find out she had cancer.

"Hi, everybody, and welcome to Adirondack Adventure!" a guy boomed out from the far side of the porch. He smiled and his dimples announced his identity before he said, "My name is Tom, and I'm going to help you with your equipment. Safety comes first out here. We want to make sure everyone has a great time."

His appearance caused a flurry of whispering among the girls. Ava snuck a glance at Sophie, who was standing next to Bethany Bridges. They whispered and laughed. Probably about the dimples, Ava thought. Sophie loved dimples.

"Let's get started." Cute-Tom showed them how to step into their harnesses and tighten the straps. Then he took them to a little practice course to go over the rules. It was pretty simple. There were two safety straps with clips attached to your harness. You always had to keep at least one of them hooked into something when you were up in the trees. That way, if you fell, you'd have one to catch yourself. So when you moved from one platform to another, you'd unhook one clip and hook it onto the new safety line, then go back and unhook the second one and move that. Always attached.

"You'll go through a safety demo now and show me that you were listening," Cute-Tom said. A few of the girls near him giggled—they'd obviously been looking more than listening—but they lined up at the edge of the course.

Ava got in line, too. When it was her turn to get her equipment checked and demonstrate her clipping and unclipping skills on the practice course, Cute-Tom tugged on her safety lines and nodded. "All right. Try out this tightrope and show me you'll be able to do this safely up in the trees. Remember, you're on your own up there."

Ava looked at him. "Aren't there guides on the platforms with us?"

Cute-Tom shook his head. "We don't have guides for every platform, so we spread out on the ground and keep a close eye on everyone from there. That's why you practice before you go up. Don't worry—we'll holler if we see you're forgetting something. Ready?"

Ava climbed the ladder, clipping and unclipping and clipping herself in, all the way up. Jason Marzigliano and Becca Case were already at the top, attached to a safety line over the wooden platform.

Jason went first, sauntering across the tightrope as if it were a foot wide instead of half an inch. Cute-Tom had said it was fine to grab the red safety line that ran over the rope, since it was good to use for balance, but Jason barely touched it.

"You make it look too easy," Becca said, laughing. She started out more slowly.

"Go ahead!" Cute-Tom called up to the platform where Ava was waiting.

Ava's stomach dropped out from under her. Go on the tightrope at the same time as somebody else? What if Becca jiggled it?

Ava unclipped one safety line and moved it ahead. Then she moved the second line. She put a tentative foot on the rope but kept her weight on the wooden platform. She could feel the line vibrating with every step Becca took.

"Come on." Eli Henderson was waiting behind her.

Ava took a deep breath, grabbed the safety line overhead, and shifted her weight onto the tightrope. It bowed underneath her, and her stomach felt as if it might drop right down to the pine-needled ground below, but she didn't fall. *Just keep going,* she thought. Keep going and there's a solid platform on the other side.

Ava took some more baby steps. She kept her eyes on the back of Becca's ponytail.

Hold on tight.

Tiny step.

Hands creep up.

Hold on tight.

Tiny step.

Hands creep up.

On some level, Ava understood that she wouldn't reach the end of the rope until next Tuesday at this rate, but she couldn't make herself move faster.

She took another tiny step, and the whole wire sank under her foot, then bounced a little. "Oh!" Ava's hands tightened on the safety line, and she looked back. Eli had stepped out onto the line and was moving fast—step, step, step—toward her.

"Woohoo!" he shouted, as the cable boinged up and down. Ava was pretty sure he was bouncing on purpose. Why would anyone *want* to feel like this?

"Hey, take it easy," Cute-Tom said from the ground, and thankfully, the bouncing settled to a gentler shake. "While you guys are up there, I want to demonstrate something, okay? Somebody fall for me."

Fall? Ava was already shaking. Even the thought of falling made her cling to the safety line for all she was worth. When she did that, the safety line dipped from her weight, and she lost her balance. She panicked and kicked at the tightrope to try to catch herself, and then it was gone, and she was dangling by her arms, kicking in the cool fall air. Ava would have screamed if she'd been able, but her heart was thumping so wildly she couldn't even suck in a breath.

"Great, now just let go," Cute-Tom called.

No way was Ava letting go. Her fingers tightened around the safety line, but it was cutting into her hands, cutting off her circulation, and the weight of her body dragged her down.

Her fingers were slipping. She couldn't breathe. She was starting to see spots—purple and green and black spots in front of her eyes—and the next thing she knew, the safety line slipped from her sweaty hands, and she fell.

But before she even had time to think "No!" she felt a tug around her middle and her legs. The harness had caught her. She was dangling in midair.

"Perfect," Cute-Tom said, pointing to her. "See how the harness catches you?"

"It's like those little-kid swings at the park," Becca said from the safety of her wooden platform.

It was, Ava realized. She was just starting to breathe again, now that she understood she wasn't dead or bleeding. Just hanging. Swinging by the harness strapped around her hips.

"Okay," Cute-Tom said, stepping up to Ava. "If you were out on the real course now, you'd need to pull yourself back up to keep going. But that tires out your arms, and since you helped me out with my demonstration, you get to cheat a little." He pulled over a small step-ladder and helped Ava find her footing. "Climb back up to the line now and you can finish."

Ava didn't want to climb anywhere, but there wasn't much else she could do with everyone staring at her. They all thought she'd fallen on purpose, as a volunteer. So she climbed back up onto the awful rope and clung to the safety line as she baby-stepped her way to the platform and ladder on the other side.

"See?" said Cute-Tom as Ava unclipped and clipped her safety lines all the way back down to the ground. "Nothing to it. Now you guys can head out on the real course."

He pointed down a trail that led into the woods. It ended at a rock wall beneath a platform at least three times as high as the one on the training course. Ava's stomach twisted. She thought she might throw up on Cute-Tom's hiking boots.

She looked at her watch—9:34—and headed for the rock wall of doom.

27

TIGHTROPES AND HULA-HOOPS

"You want to go next?" Jason Marzigliano looked at Ava.

She looked up the rock wall and caught a glimpse of the bottom of Luke Varnway's sneakers before he pulled himself up onto the platform. "No. Not even a little."

"I'll go." LucyAnn Ward clipped her safety lines and started climbing. Very slowly, Ava noticed. That was good. LucyAnn wasn't all that athletic. She was short and what Gram would call pleasantly plump. When their class ran the mile on the track, LucyAnn was the last person to finish but the only one still smiling at the end.

"Whoop!" LucyAnn's foot slipped off a rock, and she thumped into the wall when her harness caught her. "Wow, this is kinda hard," she said and started pulling herself up again.

Jason scuffed the dirt with his sneaker and turned to Ava. "So what's up with Sophie?"

"What do you mean, what's up?"

"Well, you guys are kinda friends, right?"

"Yeah." Jason didn't need to know that Sophie hadn't spoken to her since she threw herself at Jason because of the pencil.

"Do you know if she still likes me?"

Ava stared at him. Boys really must be from another planet where all the rules were totally different. "Aren't you going out with Jessica?"

He shrugged. "She broke up with me."

"Keep the line moving," one of the guides called from the walkway.

"I'll go next," Ava said, clipping herself onto the safety hooks. Even the rock wall of doom was better than talking to Jason about Sophie.

Don't look down. Don't look down, Ava thought as she climbed.

"Great job!" a voice called from below, and Ava looked down—*stupid!*—to see Cute-Tom giving her a thumbs-up. His thumb looked tiny. In fact, his whole body looked tiny. He was a long way down there. She was already pretty far up.

"Keep coming." Ava turned back to the wall and saw Lucy-Ann leaning over to look down at her. "It's easier at the top," LucyAnn said. "The rocks get closer together, see?" She pointed, and Ava saw she was right. It was doable as long as she kept breathing, but that was turning into a challenge. "You can do it. And it's really pretty up here," LucyAnn added.

Ava glanced down again. Jason had already started climbing

up behind her, so at this point, climbing down would mean climbing right onto his head, and that wasn't an option.

Hand. Hand. Foot. Foot. Ava made her body listen, and after what felt like an hour of clipping and unclipping her safety lines, she crawled onto the wooden platform and stood up. Her heart was pounding but she was here.

LucyAnn smiled at her, all red-faced and sweaty. "The first challenge is a tightrope like the one that Wallenda guy crossed over the Grand Canyon! Only, you know, this one's twenty feet up instead of a zillion. Plus we have harnesses."

"That is a very good thing," Ava said. She watched Luke walk along the tightrope. It wasn't that different from the practice line she'd crossed. This one was actually bouncing a little less. It led to a platform near the top of another tree.

"I'm pretty sure that next platform leads to a rope ladder. And my cousin whose class came last week says then there are Hula-Hoops you have to climb through."

"Wait . . ." Ava stared as Luke inched his way toward the platform at the other end of the tightrope. "I thought it was just one challenge at a time. Can't we get down in between?"

"Nope! It's one after another." LucyAnn stepped out onto the tightrope as Jason hoisted himself onto the platform next to Ava.

"So," he said, "did she say anything to you?"

"Who?" Ava said, even though she knew he meant Sophie.

"You can go on!" Cute-Tom yelled from the ground, motioning for Ava to start on the tightrope.

"She's not done," Ava called down.

"That's okay," Cute-Tom said, motioning her out again. "The bridge-type challenges can take several people at a time. Go ahead!"

So Ava clipped herself in, reached up to the safety line to steady herself, and took a tiny step out. At least it was a tiny step away from Jason and his questions. If she slid her hands forward on the safety line over her head, she never really had to let go, and somehow, that made the narrow, wobbly cable under her feet less awful.

Hands forward. Baby step. Hands forward. Baby step.

She was doing okay until the tightrope dipped under her feet.

"Whoa!" Ava gripped the safety line and held on for dear life while the cable bounced under her.

"Sorry!" Jason called from the edge of the platform.

"Can you wait until I'm done? Please?" If he didn't stop bouncing the cable all over, Ava was sure she'd throw up. And that was going to make holding onto the line and keeping her balance a million times harder.

"Keep going, you're okay!" Cute-Tom's voice drifted up to her, and Ava looked down. He was right below her, nodding encouragingly and completely unaware that he was quite possibly about to be puked on.

Ava peered over her shoulder at Jason. "Just give me a few steps, all right?" she whispered.

He nodded and thankfully stayed still until she had

hands-forward-baby-stepped herself all the way to the next platform. Ava let out a great rush of breath.

"You made it!" LucyAnn had dark spots of sweat on her T-shirt, but her eyes were full of can't-wait excitement. "And look what's next!"

Hula-Hoops. The Hula-Hoops were next. It was a tightrope like the last one, only in the middle of it, every few feet, was a Hula-Hoop that you had to climb through in order to keep going.

"Isn't this the best?" LucyAnn said, clipping herself onto the safety line.

Ava didn't answer. She wondered what kind of a horrible person had thought this was a good idea. Gram prayed for almost everybody while she watched CNN, but she always said there was a special hot place in the afterlife for certain kinds of criminals. Ava decided adventure course designers should be added to that list and have a special place there, too. Preferably one where they had to climb through flaming Hula-Hoops on a tightrope. Blindfolded.

"They're going to tell us to keep going," Jason said, nodding toward the tightrope. LucyAnn was halfway through the first Hula-Hoop, perched on it with one leg on each side, as if she were riding a horse and laughing as it bucked beneath her. "Why don't you go ahead and I'll wait until you're almost done before I start, okay?"

Ava nodded. It helped a little, knowing that the tightrope wasn't going to start bouncing under her feet right away. She was taller than LucyAnn, so she managed to baby-step up to the first Hula-Hoop, hold the safety line, and carefully step through it, one quiet, unbouncy foot at a time, to the other side. She did that again and again, and it took a while, but she made it across.

LucyAnn had already set off on the next challenge—a swinging bridge with planks that got farther and farther apart the closer you got to the end. LucyAnn had to jump from plank to plank for the last few steps.

"Woohoo!" she called from the next platform. "That one was a doozy!"

A *doozy. Just great*, Ava thought as she took the first step. It started off better than the tightropes, at least. But after the first dozen steps or so, there was no more baby-stepping on this bridge. The planks were far enough apart that Ava had to take big, open steps. She tried to land in the middle of each plank so it wouldn't wobble, but once she put her foot down too far to the right and the whole bridge tipped. She tightened her hands around the safety cable over her head and pulled herself up, back to center, then waited, taking shaky breaths until the bridge stopped tipping and her heart stopped trying to burst out of her body.

The last two steps were terrifying. Ava didn't have to jump like LucyAnn, but she did have to take such a big step that she panicked and lost her balance and had to pull herself up by the safety line. She stood there, legs spread in a half split high up in the air until the bridge stopped swinging and she could make herself step forward again.

"Great job!" LucyAnn said, grinning.

"All clear!" Luke shouted from the other end of the next crossing.

"Bye!" LucyAnn called, and jumped off the platform. Ava almost screamed until she realized it was one of the long zip lines. LucyAnn had already attached her pulley-thing and clipped her safety lines. Now, she was flying through the trees woo-hooing her way to the next platform where a thick mat wrapped around the tree waited to stop her.

"All clear!" LucyAnn hollered and waved at Ava.

Ava looked down at the pulley-thing attached to her belt. She'd been listening when Cute-Tom told everybody how to use it—she really had—but what if she did it wrong? How smart was it, really, to send a bunch of kids up in the trees to attach their own safety stuff when they could die if they did it wrong? This was exactly the kind of thing you'd expect from a person who thought it was a good idea to put Hula-Hoops on a tightrope.

"Remember how to do it?" Jason asked her.

"I think so." Ava attached her first safety line. She unclipped her pulley from her belt, clicked it into place on the wire, and attached her second line to the pulley.

"Looks good!" Cute-Tom called from below. At least the guides were paying attention.

"Ready?" Jason said. "This one looks like a blast."

I am going to hang from this cable and fly through the trees, Ava thought. It did not sound like a blast. But kids from the next group were already starting to arrive on their platform.

"Dude, are you gonna go or what?" Brett Halloway asked.

"I'm going," Ava said. But then she didn't.

She looked down at her feet on the wooden boards of the platform. LucyAnn had simply jumped. She'd tucked her feet up, let her weight fall into the harness, and let it carry her through the trees. Ava understood that was what she needed to do, too. But she couldn't make herself do it.

"You've got two lines to catch you," Jason told her, as if she didn't know that. She'd clipped them herself. And checked them. Three times.

"I know. I'm going." Ava swallowed hard. Her throat felt like tree bark.

"You're thinking about it too much," Jason said. "Just go."

Fine, Ava thought. *I'll just go.* But she didn't.

"Come on." Brett gave an impatient sigh.

"Dude, give her a minute," Jason told Brett.

Ava appreciated that, but she knew she couldn't wait forever. She held the handles at the bottom of the pulley—that's what Cute-Tom said to do so your fingers didn't get caught in anything—and leaned back so it could catch her weight. It held her. It did. It felt strong.

Just go, she thought. *Don't think. Just go.*

Go.

Ava sucked in her breath, grimaced, and jumped.

It was fast, faster than she thought. The pulley made a high-pitched whirring, zinging noise as it flew over the cable, and the wind cooled Ava's hot face. She did not feel like Peter Pan. But she was mostly doing okay until she realized she had to land on that other platform. What if she crashed into the tree? How thick was that mat? What if she didn't make it all the way there? She'd be stuck dangling out over the middle!

But before there was more time to worry, the tree came close, and Ava lifted her feet and plopped them on the platform and grabbed the safety line to pull herself up.

"You did it! You finished the gold course!" LucyAnn was waiting at the bottom of the platform. The zip line had taken them lower, so there were just a few ladder rungs to the ground. Dirt and pine needles had never felt so good under Ava's shoes.

"Silver is next," LucyAnn said, pointing to another rock wall, higher than the first one.

"That was all part of the *first* course? All those things we just did?"

LucyAnn nodded. "Isn't this the best?"

Ava stared at the new rock wall. Just because she'd survived the gold course didn't mean she'd survive silver and whatever awful color came next. Five courses. There were five courses, and she'd only done one.

Ava looked back toward the reception area and saw Mr. Avery sitting at a picnic table next to a couple of kids.

LucyAnn followed her gaze. "Looks like Leo and Alex decided to call it quits after gold."

Ava's heart jumped. She could do that, too. She could be done! She looked at LucyAnn. "I think I'm going to call it a day now, too."

"Really?" LucyAnn's mouth dropped open. She looked back up at Luke and Jason climbing down the ladder. Luke burped, and Jason cracked up. "Come on, you can't leave me with these boys."

Ava looked at the picnic tables. Leo and Alex looked kind of bored. But they looked safe. Safe was good. "Sorry, this isn't really my thing."

"But you did so great on the first one."

"Yeah, but it took me forever to cross that stuff." As soon as Ava said that, she realized she had no idea how long it had taken. It felt like forever, but when she looked at her watch, it was only 11:30.

11:30. Mom's appointment was in an hour and a half. Ava wondered if Mom was worried. Probably not. It was just a regular exam—something she did every year. But this one was going to be different. Ava's throat tightened, and she felt her breath coming quicker.

She looked back at the gold course. It had scared her but not like this. The adventure course made her a different kind of scared. A wobbly tightrope, heart in your throat, blood pumping, fresh air, and smell-of-leaves scared. This Mom-worrying scared . . . Ava took a shaky breath. *This* kind of scared was so big it felt like it might suffocate her if she sat down at that picnic table and let it catch up with her.

If she kept going, it couldn't do that. She'd be scared of

swinging logs and tightropes instead, and by the time it was over, her mom's appointment would be done and the pencil would have been wrong and she wouldn't have cancer after all. Not if Ava finished the course.

"Okay," Ava said, "let's do silver."

28

PENCIL FAIL?

Ava started up the new rock wall without looking at her watch again.

At the top, she crossed another tightrope and another hanging bridge. She inched her way across two long, skinny balance beams suspended by chains. They swung back and forth the whole time, but she kept moving until she made it to the platform on the other side.

LucyAnn was there, with her safety lines ready to go. But there was no bridge to the next platform. There was no tightrope or balance beam. Just a simple wooden swing, suspended by two ropes. It was like the one behind Anderson's general store. But there was no way they could swing high enough or far enough to get to the other side. Even if they could, what were they supposed to do? Jump and try to make it to the platform?

"How are we supposed to get over there?" Ava said.

"Luke just went and it's awesome," LucyAnn said. "Watch!" All at once, she reached for the ropes and jumped off the platform onto the swing. "Woohoo!"

The swing flew across the clearing, zipping along a cable that Ava hadn't seen before. When LucyAnn got to the other side, she jumped off onto the platform, unhooked her safety lines, and stepped out of the way. "All clear!"

Without LucyAnn's weight on the swing, a counterweight under the platform pulled it back until it was swaying gently in front of Ava.

Ava looked at the swing.

She looked at her watch.

12:30. Her mother was probably leaving for the doctor's office now. What if the pencil was right? Would they be able to tell if the cancer had spread?

"This one looks cool," Jason said as he stepped from the balance beam onto the platform behind her. "Want me to go first?"

"No, that's okay." If Ava stayed, she'd think too much, and even flying through the trees on a swing of doom was better than thinking about her mom. She clipped her safety lines, stepped onto the swing, and rode it to the other side.

"On to the pink course now!" LucyAnn said after they'd both climbed down the ladder.

The pink course started with a swinging bridge, and that was okay. Then there was a tightrope and a short zip line. Ava was starting to get the hang of those, and they were fun if you could convince yourself that flying through the trees really fast wasn't a horrible idea.

After the zip line, there was a tightrope with punching bags suspended over it every few feet. LucyAnn was edging her way across. Every time she got to one of the punching bags, she'd grab onto the safety cable and lean way back, then scoot past it and push it out of her way. When she did that, the punching bags swung and tried to knock her off the tightrope. Because Hula-Hoops made life too easy, apparently. Ava cursed the course designer again.

But she made it across with her heart pounding and felt strangely powerful when she looked back. *Take that, punching bags,* she thought. *Take that, jerky adventure course designer.* Ava followed LucyAnn through two more challenges—another balance-beam thing and a net that you had to climb through.

"One course left—here we come, red!" LucyAnn let out a war whoop and charged down the wooded path to the ladder that started the red course. At first, the course didn't seem that much harder than pink—just higher—and since Ava didn't look down, she could pretend she was just doing more practice tight-ropes and beams.

But the next challenge was a series of awful swinging poles that looked like pogo sticks. Every time Ava stepped onto a new pogo-stick-thing, it started swinging like crazy and she hugged it for dear life until it stopped. Then she reached out and pulled in the next one. Over and over, until finally, there were no more poles. Ava stepped onto the platform just in time to see Lucy-Ann leap onto a skateboard and ride it across a tightrope to the next tree.

"All clear!" LucyAnn called as the riderless skateboard flew back toward Ava. She clipped her safety lines and waited for it to stop so she could get on. But it didn't make it all the way to the platform. Ava stretched her foot out a little but couldn't reach it. She scanned the ground for someone to come fix it, but Cute-Tom was nowhere in sight.

"Come on!" LucyAnn called from the far platform.

"It's broken," Ava yelled. "I can't reach it."

LucyAnn laughed. "It's not broken. You have to jump!"

Ava looked at the skateboard. *Sure,* she thought. *Jump.*

The skateboard was about three feet away. Ava could jump that far, but she'd never jumped that far onto a thing that was then going to fly across a tightrope.

Jason had two pogo sticks left before he got to the platform. If Ava waited, she could let him go first. She looked at her watch.

1:02.

Mom would be at the doctor's office by now, probably in one of those crinkly paper gowns. Ava's stomach tightened. The pencil *had* to be wrong. It had to be. It was wrong before, about Jason liking Sophie, wasn't it? The question gnawed at her heart until Ava did the only thing she could do to forget about it.

She jumped.

The skateboard nearly flew out from under her when she landed, but she flailed her arms and leaned forward. It wasn't slowing down as it approached the next tree, not at all. She was going to have to jump again, onto the platform, but before she could make her legs move, the skateboard banged into the platform and threw Ava forward.

The mat wrapped around the tree would have stopped her, but she fell hard onto her knees on the platform instead. When she reached out to stop herself from hitting her head, her hands scraped over the boards, too.

"Are you okay?" Jason yelled from across the clearing.

"Yeah!" Ava called, even though she was only kind of okay. When she caught her breath enough to stand up, her hands were scratched, and both knees were bleeding. She unclipped her safety lines and moved to the other side of the platform. "All clear!" she called.

While Jason attached his safety lines, Ava took a deep, shaky breath. She wasn't ready to keep going. She wasn't ready for anything.

She looked at her watch.

1:05

When Ava got home, it would be done. Mom would know. Maybe she'd even know what percentage of people with her kind of cancer survived. They talked about that on *Boston Med* all the time. A forty percent survival rate, or a twenty percent survival rate. Sometimes worse. What had the pencil said about the kind of cancer her mom had? And who knew if it was even true?

Ava sat down on the platform and tucked her scraped-up knees to her chest. She was tired. Her arms hurt and her hands burned and her scraped knees were throbbing, and her pounding, racing heart couldn't keep it up much longer. Maybe the pencil would be wrong. Maybe her mom didn't have cancer at all. It was wrong before. About Jason liking Sophie. Wasn't it?

Jason jumped from the skateboard just before it hit the platform. That was apparently how it was supposed to work.

Ava stared at him. *Had* the pencil been wrong?

"Whoa!" Jason looked at Ava's bloody knees. "They probably have a first aid kit at the reception area. There's only one more obstacle and then we're done."

What if the pencil hadn't been wrong at all?

"Did you used to like Sophie?" Ava asked.

"Huh?"

"Did you used to like Sophie?"

Jason tipped his head and looked down at Ava. "I do like Sophie. That's why I asked you if she was still into me."

"But you were going out with Jessica. Before that, like two days before, did you like Sophie?"

"Well, yeah. I've had a crush on Sophie since I moved here. But then Brady told me Jessica liked me and she's pretty cute, so . . ." He shrugged. "We broke up, though, so if Sophie likes me, that would be great."

Ava wanted to scream. She wanted to shove Jason off the platform.

The pencil hadn't been wrong. The pencil was never wrong.

Mom had cancer. If she didn't know for sure already, she was about to find out.

29

TEN SURVIVORS

"Let's get moving," Cute-Tom called up. "This is the final challenge for you die-hards. Everybody else is wrapped up, and the buses are getting ready to take you back to school."

Ava took a deep breath and stood up.

Cute-Tom's eyes went wide when he saw her knees. "Whoa, you okay?"

Ava didn't look at him. She just started hooking her safety lines. "I'm fine."

She wasn't. It didn't matter. Her bleeding knees could keep on bleeding and her hands could keep on burning and none of it mattered because when she got home, her mother was still going to have cancer and she was going to have to walk into the house and hear about it, and she'd never be fine again. She just wanted to get off this course and curl up into a ball and pretend none of it was real.

Ava looked at the last crossing. It started with another swing.

No, not a swing. A log hanging from two ropes. There wasn't even a flat surface to step on. And then, about a foot away, there was another hanging log, longer than the first one and perpendicular to it, so you'd have to walk along it like a balance beam. And then another small log-swing . . . another balance-beam log . . . four . . . five more before the next platform.

Ava let out a sharp sigh and stepped onto the first log.

It swung forward as if it were a living creature that wanted her off, a bucking bronco in some nightmare tree rodeo. Ava lost her balance and had to grip the ropes to keep from falling. She held on so tight that the rope fibers felt like a thousand little needles poking into the raw scratches on her hands. Her knees were shaking so much the swing wouldn't stop moving. Finally, it slowed down enough that Ava could breathe.

Ava looked at the next log. There was no way she could do this eight more times.

She looked back at the platform, where Jason stood. He gave her a thumbs-up, but he looked just as terrified as she felt.

Ava looked down at Cute-Tom, and tears burned her eyes. Tears for her stinging hands and the pencil that was always right and her mom, who knew the truth by now—and no amount of running away or tightrope walking was going to keep it from being real. "I want to get down."

"But you're doing great!" Cute-Tom called up.

"I'm done. I want to get down."

"Come on, Ava! You can totally do this!" LucyAnn looked up at her from the ground. "Only eight people made it all the way to the end so far, and if you and Jason both make it, you'll be nine and ten!"

"What?" Ava was so surprised she forgot for a second that she was standing on a swing a million miles up in the air. She looked out at the clearing by the reception area, where pretty much everybody else was hanging out drinking water and eating granola bars. Ava had noticed that things had gotten quieter on the course, but she figured it was because everybody else was faster. "None of those people finished the course?"

"Like I said, there were eight. James Marino, Tyler Choe, Ivy Ordway, Marissa Powers, Annika Rock, and the Mason twins. And me." LucyAnn grinned up at Ava. She wore the dirt on her face like a badge of honor.

"Did everybody else have to get rescued?"

"Some did. The rest just decided they were done after the pink course." LucyAnn took a swig from her water bottle. "That was the one with the punching bags."

Before Ava could finish processing all that information, Sophie came jogging up to Cute-Tom in the clearing. "Mr. Avery sent me to see how many people were still out so we can tell the bus drivers when—Ohmygosh, Ava!" Sophie's mouth dropped open when she saw Ava on the swing. "You're doing *red*?"

"Yeah," Ava said. How had she missed the fact that people

were bailing out after the pink course and that was just fine? She could have skipped the skateboard of doom and she wouldn't be stuck on this swing if only she'd paid attention.

"That's awesome!" Sophie looked up at her as if she were levitating, as if Sophie couldn't believe it was Ava—nervous, scared-of-everything Ava—here on the red course. And almost done, too.

"Thanks." Ava couldn't quite believe it either. But there she was. And Sophie's name hadn't been on LucyAnn's list of finishers. "Did you quit after pink?"

Sophie shook her head. "I got knocked off that one with the punching bags and didn't have enough arm strength to pull myself back up, so I had to get rescued. But even that was kinda fun." She tipped her head toward Cute-Tom and smiled like crazy. "Anyway, you totally have to finish now. You're almost there!"

"Yeah!" LucyAnn called up. "You can do it, Ava!"

Ava looked at them. She looked out at the clearing, at all the people who hadn't finished. She'd made it farther than any of them. And her mom . . . her mom would be so proud if Ava could do it. Ava swallowed hard. Her mom probably needed that today.

"Go, Ava, go!" Sophie started chanting, but Ava shook her head.

"You can't do that. It'll freak me out. Just . . . be quiet, okay?"

Ava could feel everyone's eyes on her. She took a deep breath and then another one. Then she lifted one foot slowly from the swinging log and stretched it out toward the next one.

It didn't reach.

Ava pulled her foot back. She needed that log closer.

But she couldn't pull it closer without letting go of the ropes that were keeping her from falling off the log of doom. And she couldn't do that.

She tried holding the rope in the crook of her right elbow so she could get the next one with her hand. But her arm was all cramped and tucked in and it didn't go far enough either.

She stretched out her foot again.

It still didn't reach.

She pulled it back.

She started to reach out with her hand, but as soon as she let go of the first rope and felt the air on her scratched-up palm, she panicked and grabbed the rope again.

She looked down.

"You can do it," Sophie said quietly. She nodded up at Ava. "You so can do this."

"I can't reach," Ava said. She'd tried everything. "I want to get down."

"You can. It's not that far," Cute-Tom said, matter-of-factly. "But you have to let go of that rope to get the next one."

Ava stared down at him. "Let go?" She couldn't let go. If she let go, she was going to freak out and then lose her balance and flail all over the place and the log would fly out from under her and she'd fall and then—and then what? And then the harness would catch her. Like it had on the practice course. That was

pretty much the worst thing that would happen. And with everything else going on, all of a sudden, it seemed like that might be
survivable.

"Go on. Let go," Cute-Tom said. "You have to let go before you
can reach."

Ava took a deep breath and made her right hand unclench.
She held it close to the rope for a few seconds, feeling the breeze
cool the scratches on her sweaty palm.

And then she reached.

She reached out for the next rope, and before she could even
think about it, she was stepping onto the balance-beam log and
bringing her other hand forward. The log started swinging like
crazy and made Ava's stomach do flips. She held on so tight she
thought the ropes might burn right through her hands, but
she didn't let go.

She waited.

Little by little, the swinging log stopped jerking back and
forth and just swayed a little bit, and then a little bit less.

Ava baby-stepped forward to the end of the log.

She let go of the rope.

And reached.

She pulled the next log in and stepped onto it and held her
breath, hanging on until the awful swinging stopped.

Now do it again, she told herself. *Let go. And reach.*

She did. Again. And again. And again.

On the second-to-last log, Ava stepped too far forward and

her foot slipped off the front of the log, but she caught herself and used the ropes to pull herself back up. She didn't fall. She didn't need the harness.

She let go one last time, reached for the safety line, and stepped onto the platform. Everybody below her burst out cheering and clapping. Ava had forgotten they were there. For a while—how long? Two minutes? Five minutes? Ten? It didn't matter. For a while, it had been just her and the swinging logs.

Ava looked back at them, still swaying in the breeze. Her heart wouldn't stop pounding. What if she'd slipped? What if the cable hadn't held her? What if she'd fallen all that way to the rocky ground?

But none of those things had happened, Ava thought, as she climbed down the last ladder.

She'd done it.

She'd let go. And reached. And made it across.

And she was fine. Better than fine. She felt like she could tackle anything.

She looked at her watch.

2:05.

Maybe she'd even be able to handle the news she knew would be waiting when she got home.

30

PLAY LIKE JOHNNY

Ava sat with Sophie on the bus ride back to school.

"So things are a lot better because I saw Jessica at lunch, and I told her that somebody told me that Jason liked me—I didn't tell her it was a pencil because how weird is that—but I told her I had no idea they were going out or I totally wouldn't have gone near him. And she said that was okay because she broke up with Jason anyway because she found out Brady Tremont wants to go out with her. And he's cuter and an eighth grader. So then right after you finished that thing with the logs, I went up and said hi to Jason and he asked if he could call me later, and I said yes, so it looks like we might get together anyway."

"Well, that's good." Ava looked out the window for a few seconds. Almost all the leaves had blown off the trees. She turned back to Sophie. "How come you were mad at *me?*"

"I'm not mad at you!" Sophie's eyes went all big. "I was going to sit with you on the bus this morning, but you were already sitting with somebody."

"You *were* mad. Right?" Ava looked at Sophie and raised her eyebrows.

"I was really mad at your pencil. And it's weird to be mad at a pencil so I guess I kind of took it out on you." Sophie sighed. "You know how I am. Whether I'm happy or upset or whatever, sometimes I get so hyped up I don't even know what I'm thinking anymore and then I do things like decide to open crazy shopping businesses or ask out other people's boyfriends or run away from my best friend. And usually, *you're* the person I talk to about everything. You're the one who settles me down."

"Really?" Ava had never thought of herself as the stable one.

"Really. But this time, you were all wrapped up in it with the pencil and everything, so . . ." Sophie shrugged. "I'm really sorry."

"It's okay," Ava said. *Forgiveness is an attribute of the strong,* she thought. She was feeling strong today. And she was glad to have Sophie back. She was going to need a friend. But she didn't tell Sophie about the pencil's latest news. Not yet. She wanted to go home and see how bad it was and then—then she'd figure out what to do next.

Ava's dad was supposed to pick her up after the field trip, but his pickup truck wasn't in the school parking lot when the bus got back, so Ava went inside to wait. She got her books from her locker and headed for the bench by the front door, but Sophie called to her. "Hey, where's your saxophone?"

Jazz tryouts.

Jazz tryouts were today.

"It's in my band locker. But I can't go to tryouts," Ava said. "I have to go home. My dad's picking me up."

Sophie peered out the school's glass doors to the parking lot. "I don't see his truck. I'm going down for my tryout now. Call your dad and tell him you're coming, too."

Ava shook her head. "I really can't." But calling was a good idea. Maybe Dad forgot with everything going on. He had to have talked to Mom by now. "I'll call you later." Ava headed for the office.

"Hello, Ava!" Mrs. Zuckerman smiled over the counter.

"Hi, Mrs. Zuckerman. May I please use the phone to call my dad for a ride?"

"No need," she said. "He called not five minutes ago and left a message that he's busy this afternoon, but he'll pick you up at four. After jazz tryouts."

"How does he know about jazz tryouts?" Ava blurted.

"Parents have a secret sixth sense." Mrs. Zuckerman wiggled her eyebrows. "Also, because Miss Romero came by the office to call your house when you didn't show up for the auditions right away. She'd already spoken to your dad when I told her the field trip bus was running late. She said she'd wait for you in the band room, so everything's good."

No. Everything wasn't. But Ava knew that she wasn't going

to get out of tryouts now. "Thanks," she told Mrs. Zuckerman and headed for the band room.

"There you are! We were getting ready to send out a search party." Miss Romero motioned Ava toward the instrument lockers. "Get yourself tuned up, and you can play next." She turned back to talk Sophie through a tough section on her drum solo.

Ava took out her saxophone and put a reed in her mouth while she put the pieces together. Her scraped-up hands stung every time she touched something, and her arms were sore from hanging on so tight all day. She was tired, so tired of worrying. She just wanted to get home and hear the news and cry. But Dad wasn't coming for another half hour, and she knew from the adventure course that doing something was better than doing nothing. So she'd play.

"Which song did you decide to do?" Miss Romero asked Ava as Sophie waved and headed down the hall to her locker.

Ava waved back and shuffled through her sheet music. She'd accidentally brought Grandpa's Johnny Hodges song along with the jazz tryout pieces. "I practiced two of them." She sat down in front of the music stand. "I tried the *Titanic* one and—" She stopped herself from saying "the one you like better" because Miss Romero wasn't supposed to know that. "And this one." She held up the Thelonious Monk music.

Miss Romero nodded. "Give them both a shot, if you'd like. I'll listen and take some notes and we'll talk after, okay?"

Ava nodded, turned to the first page of that "Straight, No Chaser" song, and started to play. She knew how it was supposed to go—*Ba-da-ba-do-BA, ba-da-ba-da-ba-do-BA, ba-da-ba-do-BA, ba-da-ba-do-BA-WAH*—but she couldn't make the notes feel quick and sassy. Ava's version sounded stumbly and garbled. She felt bad for putting Miss Romero through all three pages, but she forced herself to the end.

"Okay, not bad," Miss Romero lied.

"It was awful."

"Well, it's a tough song," she said, "and I can tell you made a go of the dynamics, which is great. But why don't you try the *Titanic* song, too, so you get to show a different style, okay?"

Ava sighed. It was only a quarter to four. She switched the music and started playing, but all she could think about was Leonardo DiCaprio with icicles hanging off his eyebrows and somehow that made her think of her mom and chemotherapy, even though chemotherapy had nothing to do with icicles. Ava stopped in the middle of a measure and put her saxophone down.

"Is it okay if I play something else?"

Miss Romero frowned. "Like what? We did have set choices for the tryouts, so I'm not sure I can—"

"It doesn't matter if I get to try out or not. It's fine if I can't do jazz band. I just—I need to play something else right now. Please?"

Ava blinked fast to keep her tears inside. It mostly worked.

Miss Romero's face softened, and she nodded. "Sure. Go for it."

Ava pulled the Johnny Hodges song from the bottom of the pile. She didn't look up at Miss Romero's face to see what she thought of it. It didn't matter. Ava needed to play this one for herself. She needed to play like Johnny. When she'd been alone in her room it made her feel better. Not all the way better but a little looser, like she wasn't about to explode from the inside out. She needed it to make her feel that way now.

She played the song from start to finish, without looking away from the music. She played for Johnny Hodges and for Grandpa and for Mom. But mostly, she played for herself. She let the notes carry her, let her fingers ride the keys, let herself be lifted up by her own breath blowing through the horn.

She tried as hard as she could to forget she was Ava, to forget she was a tired, scared girl with scraped palms and bandaged knees and a mom with cancer. She tried to be someone else—someone who played and didn't worry, not about a thing. All the way to the last *Bah-waaahhhhh* . . .

Then she put her saxophone down. She was only Ava again. But not tied up quite so tightly inside. And that helped.

"Ava, that was . . . that was amazing!" Miss Romero took a deep breath as if she could draw in whatever was left of those notes, hanging in the air. "Just beautiful."

"Thanks."

And then someone started clapping.

Two someones, Ava saw, when she turned around.

Her parents were standing in the doorway.

31

CANCER. AND COOKIES.

"How was your doctor's appointment?" Ava asked as soon as they got in the car to go home.

Mom didn't answer right away. She looked across the front seat at Dad. He nodded at her, just a little.

"It was fine," Mom said. Then she turned in her seat to face Ava. "But they did see something that concerned them, so I had to go to a different office to have an ultrasound. That's why we're late. I also have to go back for a biopsy. Do you know what that is?"

"Kind of." Ava knew exactly what it was. She'd read all about breast cancer on that website. After something showed up on a mammogram, doctors did a biopsy, where they take a sample of tissue to check and see if it's cancer. Ava wished she could just fast forward all this; she already *knew*. "It's to find out if you have cancer."

Her mom hesitated, then nodded. "The doctor says it may not be. And if it is, they've caught it early. Very early and that's good. I don't want you to worry."

"When's the biopsy?"

"Tomorrow morning," Mom said. "They had a cancellation, so it's right away." She hesitated again. "I'd like to wait until after that to talk with Marcus and Emma, okay? They didn't even know I had this appointment today, and I don't want to worry them if it's nothing."

Ava forced herself to say okay, even though she knew it wasn't nothing.

"Good," Mom said and nodded quickly, changing gears. She complimented Ava again on her song in the band room, then asked about the adventure course and applauded when Ava told her she'd finished.

"Just like Christopher Robin told Winnie the Pooh," Mom said, "you're braver than you believe . . ."

For once, her mom got the quote right. "And stronger than you seem," Ava joined in, "and smarter than you think." She smiled, but her eyes welled up, and she had to turn toward the window. It was going to be a long couple of days. Her mom would need to remember those words, too.

The pencil wasn't wrong.

The pencil was right.

Mom's biopsy the next day not only confirmed she had cancer but agreed with the pencil on the exact kind—stage 1B breast cancer.

Just the word "cancer" made Ava's whole body feel like mush, but Mom dished out the news along with gravy for the mashed potatoes at dinner, as if she were talking about what book she wanted to read next instead of what kind of cancer treatment she was going to get.

"The doctor says they can do a lumpectomy—where they only remove the actual lump—so I'll be meeting with the surgeon in two weeks and most likely having surgery next month," she said. "After that, I'll probably need to have radiation and chemotherapy to make sure it doesn't come back."

"Next month is a long time to wait, isn't it?" Marcus said.

Emma's forehead wrinkled. "Can't they make you better sooner?"

"It's actually okay," Ava said, and reached over to put a hand on Emma's shoulder. She figured she'd had longer to get used to this whole cancer thing; she could help now. She looked at Marcus. "I was reading some stuff, and the kind of cancer Mom has doesn't spread fast at all, so nothing's going to happen in a month. And the treatment has an incredibly high success rate." She turned back to Emma. "That means it's easier for the doctors to help her get better."

"You need to thank your health teacher for me," Mom told Ava.

"What?"

"Your health teacher? The one who gave you the homework to ask about doctor visits?"

"Oh!"

"I might have put off that appointment for the field trip if you hadn't been so adamant about it." Mom poured some dressing on her salad.

"Yeah." Ava felt a flood of relief. She'd been wondering when her mom would ask why she'd been so freaked out about the appointment, how she could have known about the cancer before the doctors or mammogram technician. But Mom had no clue. She thought Ava was just being her usual neurotic, *Boston Med*–obsessed self. Like the time she'd been sure the bug bite on her knee was really flesh-eating bacteria. "For once, I worried about the right thing."

"Well, you can stop worrying now. We're taking care of this, and I'm going to be *fine*."

"Are you going to be in the hospital?" Emma-My-Name-Is-Turpentine asked.

"For a day or two, yes," Mom said.

"Can I come see you there?"

"Definitely."

"Will they have Jell-O? In my book about hospitals, there's Jell-O."

Mom laughed. "I can ask about that."

"Good. And I'll make you a name tag so the nurses know

who you are." Emma nodded as if that took care of everything and started digging out canals for the gravy in her mashed potatoes.

"So . . ." Mom sat down and started cutting her chicken. "What else is going on with everybody this week?"

Marcus talked about his egg-drop challenge in physics class, and Emma talked about how somebody stole Nebraska out of the fifty states puzzle in their classroom—"There's a HUGE hole in the middle and it's never going to be finished now"—and Dad said he was thinking about baked goods again.

"They've got this world-famous six-pound cinnamon roll in Longview, Washington," he said. "I was thinking we could have a foot-long chocolate-chip cookie or something."

"Yeah, but cookies are round," Marcus said. "It'd have to be the world-famous chocolate-chip cookie with a one-foot diameter."

"Hmm." Dad took a bite of his chicken and chewed thoughtfully. "That's a lot to say. It doesn't have the same ring to it as foot-long. What do you think, Ava?"

"I . . . I don't know." She'd been staring—just staring at them all, sitting around the dinner table eating mashed potatoes and wiping gravy off their mouths and talking about everyday things as if the cancer wasn't sitting there with them.

How were they supposed to get through this when Emma was going on and on about missing Nebraska and Marcus and Dad were arguing over geometric measurements?

"Personally," Mom said, "I'd rather see a five-pound brownie."

"Yum!" Emma squealed, and everyone laughed. Even Ava.

The world was still turning. Mom had cancer, and it was awful and scary, but there were still dinners to eat and dishes to clear and math tests to take. And this—all this talking about world-famous baked goods and eating and laughing together, just like always—was exactly how they were going to get through it. Ava couldn't imagine any other way.

32

LIKE A MAGIC TOUCH

The world kept on turning, through Tuesday night when Sophie came over for cookies and Ava told her the news. Sophie promised to be there no matter what. Ava didn't need to check with the pencil to know that was the truth.

The world turned right into Wednesday morning, so Ava got up and got ready for school. When she went down for breakfast, she found her parents with serious faces in the kitchen. Emma wasn't downstairs yet, and Marcus had left early for a math club meeting.

"What's wrong?" Ava asked.

It was a dumb question, she realized. *Cancer* was wrong. "Sorry, I mean—"

"Grandpa's not doing that well," Dad said. He looked at Mom. "We're going over to see him this morning before work."

Ava looked at the calendar. It was family night. "Aren't we all going later?"

"We are," Dad said, "but we wanted to check in this morning, too, just for a little while. I'll still be at the store when you get home."

"What's wrong with him?"

"Nothing new," Mom said and put a plate of toast in front of Ava. "He's old, and his heart has been failing for a long time."

Ava picked up her toast and scraped a burned edge off the crust. "Is it failing more now?"

"It seems that way." Mom pressed her lips together and started peeling an apple.

"Should I go with you?" Ava felt like she should, like she should play that song for him. It was all he'd wanted when she'd asked the pencil, to hear Johnny Hodges in concert again. Ava knew she was no Johnny Hodges, but she was getting better.

"No. We just have to check in with him." Mom sounded impatient, like it was Grandpa's fault his heart was failing. She cut the apple into perfect, equal slices and put them on Ava's plate. "And you need to go to school."

Ava looked up at her mom's strained face. And suddenly, she remembered what else the pencil had said about Grandpa. What he wanted even more than he wanted to hear Johnny Hodges. *He wants your mother's forgiveness.*

"You shouldn't be mad at him," Ava said quietly.

"What?" Her mother made a face. "I told you before, I'm not mad at Grandpa." She sighed. "I just have a thousand things to do today. This wasn't in my plans, but obviously, we need to stop by and we're doing that."

Ava looked up at her mom. She was biting the skin around her thumb, the way Ava did when she was anxious. "I know," Ava said quietly. "I know about the gambling and the college money."

Mom's face shifted. Her eyes filled with surprise, then sadness. "Where did you hear that?"

"Marcus."

Mom nodded slowly. She took a deep breath, and her shoulders deflated when she let it out. "Grandma Marion left that money for you and Marcus, for your education. I still can't believe he didn't respect that. To take that money and gamble with it . . ." She shook her head. "It didn't help that he won like crazy at the blackjack tables for a few weeks. That just made him hungry for more. It was like he had the magic touch when he was in Las Vegas. And then he lost it. And lost nearly every penny in that account, too."

Ava's breath caught in her throat. Mom's words were knocking into her brain.

Magic touch.

Lost it.

Magic!

Could Grandpa have been using the blue pencil to gamble? If he had—and he'd lost it—then it would explain why he started losing. But it was crazy. The pencil only answered questions. It didn't make some blackjack dealer give you all the good cards.

"I'm so sorry." Mom sighed and put a hand on Ava's shoulder. "About what happened and about not telling you why things are tough with Grandpa and me. I guess I just wanted to let you keep thinking he was the same Grandpa who gave you butterscotch candies and played old records for you when you were little."

"He hasn't been that Grandpa for a long time," Ava said. It was true. At least on the outside. But what if that Grandpa was still inside somewhere? He still loved Johnny Hodges, just the way Mr. Ames still loved baseball and Mr. Clemson still wanted to put out fires. Ava looked at her mom. She thought about the pencil. It just didn't seem likely. And it didn't matter why he'd done it anyway. "You know, Mom . . . there are scholarships and loans and stuff to pay for college. It's okay."

"Ava, you ready?" Dad called from the door. "Sophie's waiting."

"Yep." She turned to Mom. "You know, Mrs. Galvin has a quote on her wall: 'The weak can never forgive. Forgiveness is the attribute of the strong.'"

"And?" Mom tipped her head and looked at Ava.

"And I think you're strong. That's all." Ava gathered up her last three apple slices, kissed her mom on the cheek, grabbed her backpack, and headed out into the cool November sun.

33

GRANDPA'S STORY

The blue pencil went to school in Ava's backpack, like always. But today, it stayed there, even during the math quiz. She actually had a voice in her head now—if she studied, anyway, and she had—that did the pencil's job more quietly. When Ava turned in her quiz, she was pretty sure she had every answer right.

"How's your mom?" Sophie asked as they walked to the cafeteria.

"She's fine." Ava stopped at her locker to get her lunch. "I mean, she's not fine. But right now, she just feels normal. The surgery's not for like a month and a half."

"That must be weird for her," Sophie said, as they started down the hall again. "I mean, knowing that you have cancer inside you and waiting . . . I think I'd rather not know until the day I had to have the surgery, you know? So there wouldn't be all that time to think about it."

"I know." Ava sat down at their usual cafeteria table. Boy, did she know. She'd thought about that and about how much easier it would have been for her to find out her mom had cancer when Marcus and Emma did, instead of getting the pencil's secret news and then waiting and waiting. Certain kinds of information just made you worried and sad. That's why Ava had never told Sophie what the pencil said about her dad. Sometimes, it was better not to know.

"Can I sit with you guys?" Jason Marzigliano smiled down at them, holding his tray full of pizza and milk.

Sophie giggled. "Sure!"

"Absolutely. But I just remembered I was going to help Mrs. Galvin shelve books." Ava stood up. "I'll see you in gym, Soph."

Ava didn't feel bad about leaving. Sophie would be happy to have Jason to herself—he couldn't very well ask her out with Ava hanging around—and Ava didn't need any more reminders that the pencil was always right. The library was a good place to eat lunch anyway. Mrs. Galvin would have cookies out for her helpers.

"Ava! Thank goodness you're here. I just processed a whole pile of nonfiction titles that need homes. And there's chocolate chip macadamia today." Mrs. Galvin nodded to a plate on the counter.

Ava took a cookie and read the quote next to Mrs. Galvin's computer.

A ship in harbor is safe, but that's not what ships are built for. —*John A. Shedd*

Below the quote was a picture of a ship sailing out to sea, with storm clouds off in the distance. Ava sighed. She sure wasn't in harbor anymore.

She took the first few books, headed for the 500s, and put two whale books where they were supposed to go.

"How's life?" Mrs. Galvin called over. It wasn't club day, so they were the only ones there.

"Good." Ava slid a book about honeybees onto the shelf. "Well . . . kind of good and kind of bad." She went back for more books. "We just found out my mom has breast cancer."

"Oh, Ava! I'm sorry to hear that. How is she doing?"

"She's okay. She feels fine, and it's . . . it's early, so she's going to be fine." Saying so out loud helped Ava believe it, too. "She's having surgery after Christmas."

Mrs. Galvin nodded. "I'll send lots of white light your family's way."

"Thanks." Ava wasn't sure what that was—maybe Mrs. Galvin's version of Grandma's CNN prayers—but if it was coming from Mrs. Galvin, she was sure it was good.

Ava finished shelving the nonfiction and looked for a book to check out. Mrs. Galvin had asked if she wanted one about cancer, but Ava decided she'd probably feel better if she read something funny, so they found one about a girl who's forced to join a marching band even though all she really wants is to play in this super-serious orchestra.

"I think you'll like it," Mrs. Galvin said. "On the first day, she drops the big feathery plume thing that goes on top of her band hat, and the whole band starts chanting 'chicken down!' The only way she can make them stop is to cluck like a chicken."

"That sounds horrifying," Ava said. But she laughed. It wasn't her plume, after all.

She headed to the locker room, got changed for gym, and found Sophie out on the soccer field. Mrs. Snell was a die-hard when it came to playing outside. "Bring a sweatshirt," she always said, "because we're heading out until the snow's too deep to run."

Ava was fine with that. School air always felt a little stuffy, so it was nice to get outside.

"Hey, isn't that your dad?" Sophie jogged over to Ava and pointed.

"Yep." The Andersons' car was just turning the corner toward home and the store. "They were visiting Grandpa this morning."

"Is he okay?"

"Yeah, I think so." Ava didn't really want to talk about it anymore. She just wanted to run around and clear her head. She'd figured out on the adventure course that you didn't really have time to be anxious when you were out of breath from exercising.

Ava scored a goal and assisted Sophie on another one, and it felt like no time at all had passed when the coach blew the whistle for them to go inside. Ava looked at her watch. "That was the quickest forty minutes ever."

Ava had pulled open the door and turned to hold it for

Sophie when a car driving fast—too fast—caught her attention. It was her parents, heading back toward the nursing home. Ava's heart sped up. She hurried inside to the locker room, got changed, and pulled the pencil and her legal pad from her backpack.

Where are my parents going?

"To Cedar Bay," the voice said, calm as ever.

Why are they going back?

"Because Thomas called them and told them they should come right away," the voice said.

Ava wished it would just keep talking instead of making her ask question after question.

Why did Thomas tell my parents they should come right away?

"Because," the voice said. "Hank has taken a turn for the worse."

Ava stared at her question on the page and tried to make some sense of her crazy, swirling thoughts. Grandpa was getting worse, maybe even dying. And the voice had called him Hank. Like the pencil *knew* him or something.

Did Grandpa ever have this pencil that I'm holding right now in his possession?

"Yes," the voice said. Now it sounded short. Maybe mad.

Did Grandpa use this pencil to gamble?

"Yes," the voice said again.

Ava was out of space on the page. She flipped to the next one and wrote, HOW?

"He kept a small notebook on his lap at the blackjack table and asked what the dealer's hole card was—that's the card that's facedown," the voice said. "Knowing it gave him an advantage when he decided whether to take a hit on his own hand or not."

Ava was surprised to hear that was allowed. She'd seen a TV show about casino pit bosses once, and they seemed super-strict about stuff like that.

They let you do that in casinos?

"No, they don't," the voice said. "He got thrown out as soon as the cameras caught him. But he always had a chance to win a hand or two, and then he'd move on to the next casino and start over."

So he won. A lot. But then he started losing.

And then did Grandpa lose the pencil? Ava thought she already knew the answer.

"Indeed. When he'd been thrown out of every casino in Las Vegas, he came home and planned a trip to Atlantic City. He lost the pencil before he went."

"Ava, are you coming?" Sophie was waiting by the door. "We have to get to study hall." She looked down at the pencil in Ava's hand, took in the words on the page, and shook her head, confused. "What's going on?"

"I—I'll tell you later. I promise. Go ahead, and I'll be there in a minute, okay? I just . . . I have to do this."

"Okay." Sophie shrugged and walked out, and when the locker room door closed, Ava was alone with the pencil.

Why did Grandpa keep gambling after he lost the pencil?

Ava thought she heard a sigh. She turned to the door, but Sophie was long gone. She looked down at the pencil in her hand.

"Because he couldn't stop."

Ava thought maybe she understood. Maybe it was Grandpa's version of the red shoes.

But the pencil wasn't finished. "Hank started gambling—and kept gambling even after he lost the pencil—because he was trying so hard to fill the hole in his heart after I died."

After I died?

Ava gasped and put the pencil down. She stared at it, just a three-inch nub now, resting on the wooden locker room bench.

The pencil-voice was a person. A person who had died and left Grandpa alone.

Ava reached for the pencil, her hand trembling, and wrote in shaky letters, *Grandma Marion?*

The sigh came again. This time, Ava didn't look for Sophie. She knew.

"Yes," the voice said.

Part of Ava wanted to scream and drop the pencil-ghost and run away. But the rest of her needed more answers. And she needed the pencil for that.

Why didn't you tell me whose voice this was?

"Because," the voice said, "you didn't ask."

How did you get inside this pencil?

"I am not inside your pencil," the voice said. Ava was actually relieved to hear a bit of its old impatient tone again. "As you know, I died five years ago. I was using this pencil when I had my stroke behind the research desk at our downtown library branch. And it seems I was holding on tightly enough that a sliver of my spirit seeped into the wood."

Ava couldn't move her hand fast enough to ask all the questions spilling out of her brain.

Why do you only answer certain kinds of questions? And have you been in the pencil five years?

"In response to your first question," the voice said, "I answer questions that fall within my responsibilities. When I was a reference librarian, it was my job to help people find answers to questions when answers were available. But not all questions have that kind of solution, and it's not up to a librarian to be making up answers that don't exist."

"Oh." Ava nodded. The rules made more sense now.

"Question two," the pencil went on. "I have not been *in* the pencil five years because as I told you, there is no person, dead or alive, inside the pencil. It's complicated." The voice had a frustrated tone, like Mr. Farkley trying to explain math that he was sure Ava didn't understand. "It is merely a sliver of spirit that answers certain kinds of questions."

Ava was glad. But it still seemed awful to have even part of yourself stuck in a pencil sometimes. Unless Grandma Marion meant to do that.

Did you put part of yourself in the pencil on purpose?

The voice let out a huff. "If I'd had any idea such a thing

could happen, I'd have made sure I was using a nice fountain pen when I took my last breath and not some cheap giveaway from a librarians' conference. But alas, in all the books I'd read, they neglected to mention such a possibility."

Ava couldn't help thinking about all that time the pencil was sitting in the dust under Grandpa's radiator. It must have been so boring. Unless maybe the pencil-voice got to leave when nobody was using it.

Are you in the pencil all the time? Or just when someone is asking questions?

"When no one is writing questions with the pencil, that bit of spirit is at rest." The voice paused. "But obviously, that's not the case right now. So here we are."

Here we are, Ava thought.

She looked up at the ceiling of the empty locker room, as if the real Grandma Marion's ghost might be floating up there. But there was only a water stain from where the roof must have been leaking.

That, and the pencil in her hand.

Ava tried to settle her thoughts so she could sort through them and remember what was going on before the pencil let it slip that it was actually Grandma Marion. Or part of her. Or something.

Ava flipped back through the legal pad, through the bread-crumb trail of her questions, until she got back to this one:

Why did Thomas tell my parents they should come right away?

Grandpa had gotten worse. The pencil—no—*Grandma Marion* had said so. Was he going to die? Ava couldn't imagine her mom going through that now, not with her cancer and with all the bad feelings between her and Grandpa.

Ava took a deep breath and wrote:

Is Grandpa going to die?

"Yes," the pencil said, in the same matter-of-fact tone it had used to tell her that Gram was going to die someday, too, because everybody dies eventually.

Ava let out a frustrated sigh. She'd thought things might be different now that she knew it was Grandma Marion and not some random magic pencil she was dealing with. It was her grandmother, after all. But no . . . they were apparently back to the super-strict rules about facts and no future-telling.

She wrote the next question so hard the pencil tip broke on the point of the question mark.

Is Grandpa going to die today?

The voice didn't say anything, and at first Ava thought it wouldn't, but then she heard the quiet breath again . . . as if it was getting ready to respond.

"Yes," the voice said quietly in Ava's ear. And this time, the voice was different from the one Ava had grown used to hearing—it was full of equal parts sadness and longing and joy. "Yes, he is."

The bell rang.

But instead of going to study hall, Ava dropped the pencil

and legal pad into her backpack, tossed the whole thing over her shoulder, and raced from the locker room through the gym. She ran right out the door—for once not worried about the trouble she might get in.

She could explain later.

First, she had to make sure Grandpa got his wish.

34

SAYING GOOD-BYE

Ava ran across the soccer field and down the sidewalk. She ran all the way up Champlain Street and past her house and the store, past Lucy and Ethel, who didn't even look up from their oats. She ran past Sophie's house and the empty lot, down Marshall Street and the long driveway, through the front doors of Cedar Bay.

Thomas was coming down the hall. He looked surprised to see Ava at first but then said, "Come on, kiddo. Your folks are down with your grandpa. I'll take you." And they headed down the long hallway to Grandpa's room.

"Your parents know you were coming?" he asked Ava.

"Not exactly," she said. "I thought I should . . ." She hesitated. "I wanted to say good-bye."

Thomas nodded. "Okay." He didn't tell her she didn't need to be there. He didn't tell her Grandpa was going to be all right, and she was grateful for that. She knew.

Even if she hadn't, she would have known the second she stepped into the room. Mom and Dad and Aunt Jayla and Uncle Joe were lined up in straight chairs by the window. Grandpa was in bed, pale and thin as she'd ever seen him. He reminded Ava of those fragile leaves you sometimes found in spring, wispy skeletons left over from the year before, waiting to be blown away.

"Ava!" Her mom stood up and hurried to her at the door. "You're supposed to be in school. How did you get here?"

"I walked." She realized how sweaty and rumpled she must look. "I ran, really. I wanted—I needed to come."

"Who signed you out? You can't just—"

"Alisha," Dad said softly. "She's here and that's good. Let it be."

"We were about to go find something to eat anyway," Aunt Jayla said. She stood up, gave Ava a quick hug, and left with Uncle Joe.

Mom didn't say anything else. She took Ava's hand, led her to an empty chair, and sank into her own. Her cheeks were streaked with mascara-smudged tear trails.

"Did you talk to Grandpa?" Ava whispered. She so hoped her mom's answer was yes. He looked so tired now, like maybe he was already leaving.

"I did." Mom reached out and squeezed Ava's hand. "Thank you for that. I'd like to think I would have done it on my own, but—well, thank you."

"Can I talk to him?" Ava asked.

Dad nodded and motioned her to pull up her chair. The whole room smelled like cleaning chemicals and old chicken soup. Close to the bed, those smells were even stronger, but Ava forced herself to lean in.

"Hi, Grandpa. It's me." Ava put her hand on his, but his eyes didn't open. "It's Ava. I just wanted to see you and say hi." It wasn't all she wanted, not at all. She wanted to talk to him and have him answer and ask him questions and tell him she knew about the pencil. She wanted to tell him she understood what he did—understood what happened to him, because the pencil had pulled her in the same way. She wanted to tell him it was okay. That she'd be okay and so would Marcus and Emma.

"Ava." Grandpa's voice was scratchy. He opened his eyes, then swallowed slowly, like it hurt. He looked over at her mom.

"You need some water, Dad?" Mom reached for the pitcher by the bed, but it was empty. "I'll be right back."

She left, and Ava looked at her dad. "Do you want to go with Mom for a walk?" she asked, hoping he'd say yes, even if he didn't feel like walking. Dad understood things like that sometimes.

"Sure." He kissed the top of her head. "Be back soon, Hank," he told Grandpa and headed out the door to catch up with Mom.

Ava knew she would only have a few minutes. She wasn't sure what to say first. "How are you feeling?" As soon as she said it, she wanted to pull the words back. He was dying. It was a fact or the pencil wouldn't have said so.

But he told Ava, "I'm hanging in there." His eyes looked so tired, so sad. And there was nothing Ava could say to make it better. She wished she had her saxophone.

"I'm sorry I can't play for you today," she said. "I don't have my instrument. But . . . I have something else." She unzipped the small pocket of her backpack and pulled out the pencil. "I found this." She held it up so he could see, so he could see the color and read the writing on it, even though it was a lot more used up than the pencil he'd lost.

Grandpa's eyes lit up with recognition the second they landed on the pencil, and then flickered with something else. Fear? Regret? He looked at Ava. "Where did you find it?"

"In the junk drawer at home," she said. "I guess Mom found it under the radiator when she was cleaning out your apartment." Ava looked around the sparse white room where Grandpa lived now. For a little while longer. "When you moved here."

Grandpa took a long, rattly breath. "When I first heard that voice again . . ." He shook his head a little and gazed up at the ceiling. "I miss her so much."

Ava's eyes filled with tears. She was sad for Grandpa and for her mom and the cancer and sad for herself. She was sad and confused and exhausted from all the questions and all the answers and all the questions she still wanted to ask. They were never ever going to end.

Grandpa's eyes focused on her. "You used it, didn't you?"

Ava nodded. She swallowed hard and tried to blink back tears, but they spilled out.

"Are you okay?" Grandpa whispered.

She nodded. "I think so. It's just . . ." She didn't know where to start. "It was awful, knowing some things."

Grandpa moved his hand toward hers, where it rested on the bed but didn't make it all the way there. Ava put the pencil on the nightstand and folded her sweaty hand around his cool, papery fingers.

Grandpa looked at the pencil for a few seconds. "Best for you to let it go, too, sweetheart," he whispered. Then he looked at her. "I'm sorry."

"It's okay. It is. I love you, Grandpa."

Grandpa whispered, "Love you, too," and then his eyes fluttered shut. His breathing was slower, quiet.

Mom and Dad came back with a nurse carrying a pitcher of water a minute or two later. "Sorry we took a little while," Mom said quietly. "We called Gram. She's bringing Marcus and Emma."

Ava looked up at them and nodded. "That's good." She didn't let go of Grandpa's hand.

Ava moved to the side but still didn't let go when Gram brought Marcus and Emma to give Grandpa kisses.

She didn't let go when his breathing got slower and the heart monitor summoned the nurses and they said yes, it would be soon.

She didn't let go until he was gone. With Grandma Marion again.

And then, Ava hugged her parents and cried with them.

When their tears were all cried out and it was time for them to leave, she slipped the pencil from the nightstand back into her bag and went home.

35

REACHING

That night, Ava said prayers with Gram in her bedroom. It smelled good in there, like warm peanut butter cookies, and that made Ava feel like Gram would be around baking for a long time. If that wasn't true, Ava didn't want to know.

Then she went up to bed. Mom came and started reading about Ivan, but it was a sad chapter, and she stopped less than a page in. "Okay if we skip this tonight? I've had enough tears today."

"Me, too," Ava said, and snuggled with Mom until Dad called upstairs.

"Honey? Your sister's on the phone."

"Okay if I go talk to her?" Mom asked.

"Yep. Love you."

"Love you, too." Mom gave Ava a long hug, then left and closed the door quietly behind her.

As soon as it clicked, Ava climbed out of bed and turned on

her light. The wood floor chilled her bare feet. It was getting colder and their thermostat hadn't kicked on yet. She sat down at her desk, tucked her feet up under her to keep them warm, and pulled her backpack into her lap.

She unzipped the small pocket and pulled out the pencil. She'd never forget the way Grandpa had looked at it. Like it was dangerous. Like he was afraid of what it might do, or what *he* might do if he had it again.

If Gram had found this pencil, Ava thought, she would have used it to find out all the secrets about religion and God. If Marcus had found it, he'd have discovered some new element by now or solved world hunger. But Ava? Ava had used it to feed her worries. She'd fed them and fed them and fed them until they'd shoved aside almost all the other parts of her. If her worries had been the tomato plant getting watered on the cover of that book in the library, Dad would have his world-famous largest tomato by now.

Ava looked down at the pencil. It was only a few inches long. How many answers could be left in there? Fifty? Sixty? A hundred?

Whatever it was, Ava understood it wouldn't be enough. It would never be enough.

But she had to ask Grandma Marion one more question.

I know you don't give advice, but will you help me decide what to do, just this once?

There was no answer. Ava waited, just in case the pencil was thinking, but the only sound was the radiator, finally clunking to life in the corner.

Ava looked at the pencil. It wasn't actually Grandma Marion, she remembered. Just—what had she called it?—a sliver of her spirit? Ava sighed. Why couldn't she have her actual grandmother instead? The real Grandma Marion would hug her and wipe her tears and love her and probably say all kinds of things that would make her feel better. Ava swiped her sleeve across her cheek to wipe away a tear.

Fine. If whatever part of Grandma Marion was in that pencil wanted to be all strict again, Ava could figure that out. She'd play the pencil's game.

If Grandma Marion were here, what would she tell me right now?

There was a pause, and at first, Ava thought the pencil was going to ignore her.

But it had to answer that, didn't it? It totally knew what Grandma Marion was like, since it *was* Grandma Marion, kind of. So it would know for sure what she would say if she were there, which she kind of was, even though the pencil was insisting it wasn't really her.

Ava was about to put down the pencil and go back to bed when finally, quietly, the voice answered.

"If your grandma Marion were here," it said, "she would tell you that the pencil in your hand is doing you more harm than good."

But the pencil told me about Mom's cancer, Ava wrote. What if Mom had cancer and didn't find out?

The pencil didn't answer that.

Ava tried again. What would Grandma Marion say about this if she were here?

"She would say that's no reason to keep it," the voice said. "The world already has a magical pencil to detect breast cancer. It's called a mammogram. That's what truly allowed for your mother's early diagnosis."

It was true, Ava realized. Her mom had scheduled that mammogram appointment before Ava even knew there was a magic pencil.

What else would Grandma Marion say right now if she were here?

The voice sighed, but when it spoke again, it sounded warmer, almost like a real grandmother.

"She would tell you that you need to let go . . ."

"Before you can reach," Ava whispered.

"She would tell you to treasure the people you love right now," Grandma Marion went on, "instead of worrying about when they'll be gone. She would tell you that in spite of her work as a reference librarian, she discovered that life isn't about knowing all the answers. The best we can do is to make peace with our questions, learn who we are, know our strengths, and do the best we can with the gifts we've been given while we're here."

Ava listened with tears streaming down her face, so many that she thought for sure she'd be empty soon. But she felt like she was filling up in other ways. Better ways.

"She would also tell you that she's proud of you," the voice said. "And that she loves you so very much."

Ava stopped trying to hold back her sobs and picked up the pencil.

I love you, too, Grandma Marion. A tear slipped down her cheek onto the page. THANK YOU.

The pencil didn't say anything back. After all, it wasn't a question.

◀━━━━ ▯▯

Grandpa's calling hours and funeral were on Saturday.

When it was Ava's turn to kneel on the tiny padded bench in front of the casket, she said one of Gram's prayers. She tried to imagine some of Mrs. Galvin's white light shining on him. And she whispered, "I love you, Grandpa. It's all okay."

Then she reached into her pocket and pulled out the pencil.

You couldn't even call it a pencil anymore, not really. More of a pencil stub. It probably had forty or fifty more questions left in it, at least, she thought. But what if one of them gave her an answer that sent her spinning and reeling again and then there weren't enough questions left to fix it?

It would be better to let it go on purpose, she decided.

Ava ran her thumb over the blunt tip of the pencil. She looked around to make sure nobody was watching and gave it a quick kiss, then tucked it between the soft, worn flannel of Grandpa's blue work shirt and the smooth, cream-colored satin that lined his casket. It was the kind of material Grandma Marion would have picked out, pristine and proper. But somehow it looked right next to the weathered blue fabric of Grandpa's faded shirt. Grandma and Grandpa must have been good together that way, too.

Ava felt a hand on her shoulder and turned.

"You ready to see some people?" Mom said. "They're going to open the doors so the neighbors can pay their respects."

Ava hesitated. "Just another minute?"

Mom nodded and went to rearrange the photographs on the welcome table, and Ava turned back to the casket. "Thank you," she whispered to whoever might be able to hear. She stared at the fold of fabric that hid the pencil. She thought about all the things she'd never know and fought an urge to reach in and take it back.

She took a deep breath, counting to four, held it for two counts, and let it out again. Slowly.

No. She knew she couldn't keep it.

She would try to make peace with her questions, like Grandma Marion said.

She'd let go.

After the funeral, everyone came back to the house to talk and cry and hug and eat Gram's macaroni and cheese. Gram had regular pasta instead, because of the lactose thing.

"You know, we're talking about making the world's largest brownie to get some attention for the general store," Dad told a handful of uncles and cousins who were gathered around the crockpot dishing up pulled pork.

Ava was already imagining her poor dad with a giant pan of brownies, all soupy batter in the middle and burned to a charred crisp on the edges. She handed him a roll for his sandwich. "Actually, Dad . . . I've been thinking. Maybe world-famous baked goods aren't the answer."

She'd actually been thinking a lot. Mostly, about what Grandma Marion said about being at peace with who you are, overcoming your donuts-on-fire weaknesses and knowing your strengths. Her dad's biggest strength was bringing people together and making them laugh. "I might have an even better idea for the store."

"Friendship is the only cement
that will ever hold the world
together." —Woodrow Wilson

WELCOME TO THE FIRST ANNUAL
KNOW-YOUR-NEIGHBOR FESTIVAL

Celebrating our community and
its small, locally owned businesses

ANDERSON'S GENERAL STORE

Saturday,
May 21

36

A WORLD-FAMOUS FESTIVAL

It took a whole winter of planning and phone calls, poster making and letter writing. There were more than a few moments of can-we-really-pull-this-off and lots of late-night brainstorming sessions that ended with fits of laughter and pie around the kitchen table. But no one could deny that the First Annual Anderson's General Store Know-Your-Neighbor Festival was a spectacular success.

The weather was perfect—cool, spring sunshine that promised to warm up into picnic and short-sleeves weather by early afternoon.

Ava and Sophie spent the morning helping little kids on the miniature adventure course they'd set up in the general store's front yard using equipment borrowed from school. Mr. Avery had set up the practice balance beams, and even though they didn't have the harnesses and safety stuff for a high ropes course, the short, low zip line that went from the tree to the telephone pole by the driveway was a big hit.

Marcus had cordoned off squares for Goat Poop Bingo on the front lawn. He was selling tickets at a table while Lucy and Ethel chowed down on oats, getting ready for the big event.

Emma had set up a booth right by the parking area, offering everyone name tags so it would be easier to meet new people. "If you don't want to use your real name, you can choose a different one, and we'll all call you that instead," she offered. Most people chose their real names, but Ava did see Emma's teacher wandering around, wearing a tag that read "HELLO MY NAME IS RHUBARB."

Mrs. Galvin volunteered to run a used book sale. She lured people in with her chocolate chip macadamia nut cookies and made personal recommendations for everyone, kid or adult.

Gram sold cookbooks at the next table over. Marcus helped her with the layout on the computer and she had them printed downtown. The *Anderson's General Store Cookbook* included Gram's famous mac and cheese, and she'd gotten all the old ladies at her church to share their recipes, too. Even Mrs. Dobson, who swore she'd take the secret of her butterscotch pie to her grave. So the cookbooks were a big hit.

The town council members came to help judge the First Annual Anderson's General Store Bad Baking Contest. Dad didn't enter. "That just wouldn't be fair to the rest of the community," he said. "They wouldn't have a chance." Since Dad's half-baked giant blueberry muffin and flaming donuts weren't in the running, Mrs. Finnegan from the Venerable Vinyl record store took first place with a recipe she discovered by accident.

"I hadn't planned on baking molasses-peanut-butter-raisin-fudge-lemon sugar cookies," she told the crowd, standing proudly at the microphone with her trophy, a baking sheet that Sophie and Ava had spray-painted gold. "I'd measured out all the ingredients for five different kinds of Christmas cookies, but the phone kept ringing and I forgot which kind I'd started making. So I ended up putting in everything." She took a bite of one of the cookies and grimaced, then held her gold baking sheet over her head, and everybody cheered.

Mom handled sales in the store—and sales were brisk—while Dad wandered around and personally thanked everyone for coming. He told jokes and complimented people on their bad cookies and played with the little kids and did all the things Dad did best. On one side of the store, Katina D.'s new song played from the speakers while a bunch of high school girls danced. On the other side, families lazed on spread-out blankets watching I Love Lucy episodes projected onto the wall of the shed and licking regular, scoop-shaped ice cream cones that were neither the world's largest nor the world's smallest. Everyone seemed to love them anyway.

At eleven o'clock, Ava and Sophie took a break from the obstacle course and set up their fortune-telling booth to raise money for the activities fund at Cedar Bay. It was just for fun, and after the goldenrod gall fiasco in science class, Ava insisted that their sign be honest about that.

FORTUNE-TELLING WITH MADAME SOPHIE AND THE MYSTICAL AVA*

*Madame Sophie and the Mystical Ava are not actual certified fortune-tellers or psychics. All fortunes are made up and probably won't come true unless they happen to guess right, which would be quite a coincidence.

It didn't stop people from handing over a dollar each to have their fortunes told while Ava and Sophie looked into the reflecting ball they'd borrowed from Sophie's mom's garden.

Mrs. Galvin was first in line. "Hmm . . . You are going to read an amazing book that will change your life," Ava told her.

Mrs. Galvin said, "I like that fortune. All books do that for me, even if it's just in little ways."

"Me, too," Ava said, "but some more than others."

Mr. Avery stepped up to the table and put down his dollar. "Did you get your run in yet today, Ava?"

"Not yet. I've been busy helping here." Ava had joined the school's modified track team, and Mr. Avery had let her skip the day's official practice to set up the festival. "But I promise I'm going out right after we're done." She looked down at his dollar. "Do you want your fortune told?"

"Of course!"

Sophie swept in, took the dollar, and told him, "You are going to have a terrific winning season, Coach." She put an arm around Ava. "And a new star runner, too."

He grinned. "I'm counting on it." Then he went to look at Gram's cookbooks.

Marcus was next in line. He dropped four quarters onto the table, and Sophie looked into the shiny metallic orb on the table, waving her hands over it mysteriously. "You are going to have great success in the field of science," she told him.

"Really?" He grinned.

"But you will need to dry the dishes tonight," Ava added, "even though it's not your turn, to ensure that good karma allows this prophecy to come true."

"Yeah, right." Marcus shook his head and walked away, but Ava thought he might actually do it. You could never be too careful about karma.

"I want to know my future, but I don't have any dollars." Emma stood on her tiptoes to see into the crystal ball. "Daddy says if you go ahead and do it, he'll pay for me later."

"Let's see." Ava leaned forward to look into the crystal ball. "It looks like next year, you will be the only Emma in your whole entire class," Ava whispered.

Emma's face lit up, and she ran back to her name tag booth.

"She's going to be so mad if you're wrong," Sophie said, laughing, as she watched Emma go, "especially if she uses up all those name tags." Then she looked down quickly and whispered, "Okay, don't look now, but Jason is coming. Let me handle this one, okay?"

"Okay." Ava was surprised Sophie would want to talk to Jason. "You don't like him again, do you?"

Sophie shook her head and grinned. "No. But a customer is a customer." She'd been furious with Jason since he dumped her for Gracie Madison on New Year's Eve, but she gave him a big smile when he put his dollar down on the table.

"Let's see what the crystal ball has to say about your future." Sophie waved her hands over it and frowned into it. She waved her hands some more and jumped back a little as if something she'd seen surprised her.

"What? What's in there?" Jason looked truly nervous. He obviously hadn't read the poster's fine print.

"I see . . . this is very unusual." Sophie leaned closer to the metallic ball.

"Unusual how?"

"I see a number of girls in your future," Sophie said.

"Really?" Jason's voice was hopeful. Ava had to suppress a laugh. "Who are they?"

Sophie shook her head. "It is too cloudy to say for certain. And the dollar only covers one minute, so your time is up."

"Can I give you another dollar?"

"Sure."

Jason handed over another dollar, but the crystal ball stayed cloudy. So he paid another one. Sophie waved her hands and frowned some more and shook her head.

Poor Jason was up to five bucks when Ava started to feel bad for him and kicked Sophie under the table.

"Oh!" Sophie said and looked at Ava.

"I can see it now . . . One of them is Rosa Benson," Sophie said. Rosa was a quiet flute player who was always mooning over Jason in band.

"Who are the other ones?" Jason asked.

Ava jumped in. "That's all we're going to see, I'm afraid. But know that . . . um . . . you will have success in life and love."

"Cool," Jason said, and left for the ice cream counter.

"Success in life and love?" Sophie cracked up after he was gone.

"It was the only thing I could think of to get him to leave while he still had some of next week's lunch money. You are truly evil," Ava told Sophie, but she couldn't help laughing.

"He had it coming to him. Plus it's all going to a good cause." Sophie nodded over to the chairs set up on the lawn. Thomas and Betty had gotten special permission to bring some of the Cedar Bay residents out for the day in the nursing home van that took them shopping sometimes. Mrs. Raymond was there. She'd started the day bundled in her monster trucks sweatshirt but had it draped over her shoulders now that the sun was so warm.

The jazz band wasn't performing until later, but Mrs.

Grabowski's family had brought some old Ukrainian music and set up an area for dancing. They'd done their best to dress in traditional costumes. Mrs. Grabowski could only dance for a minute or two at a time, but even when she had to sit down to rest, she looked happy, wearing Sophie's flowery, ribbony tiara and tapping her white sneakers in time with the music.

Everyone seemed to enjoy it, whether they were Ukrainian or not. Mr. Ames was there, slapping his knee. Mr. Clemson was nodding in time to the music, looking around behind him every few minutes, probably sniffing for smoke. But he must have felt comfortable; he never looked anxious for long. Mrs. Yu was sitting near Mrs. Grabowski, making the chewing motions with her mouth, nodding and tapping her feet a little, too.

"Mrs. Yu's jamming," Sophie said.

"Yeah." Ava watched her for a minute. "She looks kind of sad, too, though. I wonder why. If we still had the pencil, we could ask."

Sophie was quiet for a few seconds. "Do you miss it?"

"Sometimes."

It was true. Sometimes, she missed knowing what people were thinking, knowing she could find out what they needed and help them. She missed the comfort of knowing she wasn't going to fail a math quiz, no matter what. But studying with Mrs. Galvin was almost as good as the pencil when it came to that. And Ava's new counselor, Miss Cosgrove, was helping her with her anxiety, too. Mom and Dad had set up the first appointment after Mom's diagnosis, because even when you were stronger than you thought and braver than you believed, it helped to have some extra strategies in your pocket.

Still, there were times when Ava wondered things, like if the latest PET scan was right when it showed Mom's cancer was really, truly gone. How Gram really felt when she skipped dinner or went to bed early one night. What it meant when Jason Marzigliano's friend Noah looked at her from the percussion section during jazz band.

But Ava didn't miss the way the pencil made her need it. Like every answer gave her more questions to worry about. Like she couldn't live without it. And pencils don't last forever. Eventually, the sharpener would have ground this one down so tiny it couldn't be sharpened any more. Ava could imagine herself scraping desperately away at the wood with her fingers until they bled, trying to get the last bit of lead to give up its answers. And then what? She didn't miss that desperate, panicky feeling.

"Mostly, I'm glad it's gone," she told Sophie.

Sophie nodded. "Maybe Mrs. Yu misses your grandpa."

"I bet she does. We all do." They were quiet for a few minutes. Then a shout burst out from the front lawn, and when Ava looked up, Mr. Finnegan was jumping up and down pumping his arms in the air. Ethel had just pooped in his square.

At noon, the world-famous invent-your-own-sandwich bar opened, and Dad manned the counter, helping everybody assemble the lunch of their dreams. They ate their peanut butter-and-marshmallow sandwiches and roast-beef-mustard-double-cheese submarines and listened to the middle school jazz band play "On the Sunny Side of the Street."

Miss Romero had ordered the sheet music for the whole band right after Ava's audition, and they'd been practicing ever since. Ava had loved playing the song at her spring concert at school. She wished Grandpa had been there to hear it, but it was enough to have her mom there. The concert had been just a week after Mom's last chemotherapy treatment, so she'd worn a bright-orange scarf over her bald head. But Ava didn't mind—it made it easier to find her there in the audience, crying and smiling while Ava belted out the notes.

Scoo-ba-doo-ba-doo-wahhh . . .

Today, playing at the festival, Ava knew those notes by heart, so she didn't have to keep her eyes glued to the music. She could take in the crowd.

Mom was there, sitting cross-legged in the grass near Mrs. Yu. She'd taken a break from the store to listen. Her hair was growing back now, and she looked healthy and strong. If you didn't know her, if you hadn't seen her in the hospital or right after, you'd never guess that she'd been sick.

Ava took a quick breath and started the next riff.

Scoo-ba-doo-ba-doo-wahhh . . .

The sun was warm on her black hair, and the breeze tickled her fingers on the keys. She played her smooth Johnny Hodges notes up into the sky, for Grandpa and Grandma Marion, and out over the crowd on the general store lawn.

She played for her teachers and neighbors and classmates. She played for the Cedar Bay residents with their hidden-away memories, for Gram and Mom, for Emma carefully Magic-Markering name tags in her booth. For Dad and Marcus serving some of the weirdest world-famous sandwiches around. Seeing them all there filled her up.

Ava closed her eyes for the last, long notes.

Scoo-ba-doo-ba-doo-wahhh . . .

Everyone clapped and it broke the spell. Ava opened her eyes and took it all in.

Did she miss the pencil?

Sure.

Sometimes.

She still worried too much and wondered about things she couldn't know now.

She'd never have all the answers again.

But she had the ones she needed most.

ACKNOWLEDGMENTS

Like Ava, I am thankful for the family, friends, and colleagues who fill my world with joy, conversation, laughter, and cookies, even when I can't find all the answers I'd like.

Lots of questions pop up while you're writing a book, and I appreciate the people who helped me with those. Thanks to Angie Miller and her goats for their advice on Ethel and Lucy. Martha White and Tom Schirmer offered great thoughts on what might happen if one tried to use a pencil, magic or otherwise, in a casino.

Thanks to the Wakarusa Dime Store in Wakarusa, Indiana. I stopped there on my way to the airport after speaking at the All-Write Conference a few years ago, enjoyed some jumbo jelly beans, and have been thinking world-famous thoughts ever since. I'm also grateful for the Adirondack Extreme Aerial Adventure Park in Bolton Landing, New York. When I signed up for your sweat-and-stress-inducing obstacle course, I didn't realize I was doing research, but that stomach-dropping swinging logs challenge provided me with the exact inspiration I needed to finish Ava's story when I got home.

Remember the book Ava finds in her school library? *What to Do When You Worry Too Much: A Kid's Guide to Overcoming Anxiety* is a real book that actually does have a giant tomato plant on its cover. It's written by Dawn Huebner and was a great help to me in writing *All the Answers*. It's also a terrific resource for anyone who feels like Ava sometimes. School guidance counselors can help a lot, too.

Thanks to my critique pals and beta readers, Linda Urban, Loree Griffin Burns, Liza Martz, Eric Luper, Laurel Snyder, Jenna Ward, Bethany Ward, Meghan Germain, Michelle Germain, and Ella Messner. My agent, Jennifer Laughran, believed in Ava from the start and encouraged me to write this book, and my editor, Mary Kate Castellani at Bloomsbury, pushed me to ask the hard questions to make it a stronger story. Many thanks to cover illustrator Gilbert Ford and designer Nicole Gastonguay, and the rest of the amazing Bloomsbury team as well: Cindy Loh, Beth Eller, Linette Kim, Linda Minton, Ilana Worrell, Melissa Kavonic, Lizzy Mason, Courtney Griffin, Erica Barmash, and Emily Ritter. I'd tackle an adventure course of doom with all of you any day of the week.

And finally, to my family, Tom, Jake, and Ella, with much love—thank you for being the amazing, smart, funny people you are, for asking impossible questions, and being the answer to everything, all at once.

Read on for a sneak peek at Kate Messner's next novel, with tons of heart, a touch of magic, and a wish-granting fish!

One day while ice fishing, Charlie comes across the surprise of her life—a floppy, scaly fish that offers to grant her a wish in exchange for its freedom. She can't believe her luck . . . until she realizes that this fish has a funny way of granting wishes, despite Charlie's best intentions. Are some things too important to risk on a wish?

The Littlest Catch

"I'm thinking of a word," I tell Mom and Dad at breakfast the next morning.

Dad pushes his bagel into the toaster and looks up at the ceiling. "Vendetta?"

"Marigold," Mom says from the closet, where she's pulling out snowshoes.

"Dad wins. It was telegram."

"Ha!" Dad high-fives me on his way to get the peanut butter from the cupboard.

"Humph." Mom sets two pairs of snowshoes on the bench by the door. "How do you figure?"

"Because you could send a telegram about a vendetta, obviously," Dad says. "Nobody sends telegrams about marigolds."

"I hate this game," Mom says, laughing. The game is

totally stupid, but it's a family tradition. When I was five and Abby was eleven, we used to play the guess-what-number-I'm-thinking game. She'd tell me she was thinking of a number between one and a hundred. I'd guess five; she'd tell me if it was higher or lower, and I'd keep guessing until I figured it out. I thought it was the coolest thing ever— everything Abby did was cool—so I started bugging Mom and Dad to guess numbers. One day, I said I was thinking of a word, and everybody should guess what it was. Mom and Dad each guessed a few times before they explained there were too many words to play the game that way. But I loved the word game, so we decided everybody could guess once and whoever was closest to the word would win. After that, the word game just stuck around.

Abby even played with us from college this fall, via group text.

Abby: I'm thinking of a word.

Mom: I hope the word is study. ☺ Don't you have a test Friday?

Charlie: Diligent.

Abby: Oohhh, fancy guess.

Charlie: Vocab word.

Dad: THE WORD IS MARSHMALLOW.

Abby: Stop shouting, Dad. You're all wrong. It was jeggings. Mom wins because jeggings are comfortable study attire.

Dad tried to argue—still shouting because he doesn't know how to turn off the caps lock on his phone—that if you wear jeggings, you can eat lots of marshmallows because they're elastic. Mom said that was a stretch, and then she was all proud of her pun. (Get it? Elastic . . . a *stretch*?)

Sometimes, it's easy to decide who wins. Like if the word is dangerous, and Dad guesses dishwasher and Mom guesses mushroom, then she totally wins because of poisonous mushrooms. But it can get tricky. Once Mom and Dad argued for ten minutes over which word was closer to sunflower—flashlight or rebellious. (Flashlight won. Because of yellowy brightness.) Abby's always been the best at making a case for her guesses, but she's sleeping late again, so Dad wins the vendetta-marigold-telegram argument today.

"We're going snowshoeing in the park," Mom says, pulling snow pants from the shelf. Dad's an English teacher, and she's a part-time school nurse, so they have the whole winter break off too. "Want to come?"

"Actually, Mrs. McNeill invited me ice fishing with her and Drew."

Dad raises an eyebrow. "Wouldn't that involve going out on the ice? Last year, we couldn't even get you out skating once."

"I know. But she says we won't need to go out far. I think I'd like to try."

Mom goes to the window and glances at the thermometer. "Ten below." She makes a face as if she's calculating how much ice could have formed over a night that cold. "Okay. We'll see you back here for lunch."

"Should I ask Abby if she wants to come?"

Mom's eyes dart to the stairs and then to Dad, who grimaces and shakes his head. They've had a lot of serious kitchen-table conversations with Abby since her first semester grades showed up during vacation. I guess the grades weren't very good.

"I don't think Abby's quite ready to face the world this morning," Mom says. "Don't forget your phone. And dress warmly or you'll freeze to death."

Two sweaters, one puffy winter coat, two scarves, one pair of snow pants, one hat with ear flaps, and one pair of thick mittens later, I'm waddling across the yard to the McNeills' house. I feel like that snowsuit kid who couldn't move in the movie *A Christmas Story*, but it's too cold to be wearing anything less. The sun's out, though, so hopefully it'll warm up to zero soon.

Mrs. McNeill practically lives with Drew and his parents during fishing season. She and Drew are already out in his yard, getting fishing stuff ready. Drew tears open a package of Pop-Tarts and offers me one.

"What kind is it?" I ask.

"Strawberry. Duh."

"Thanks." When you've been friends as long as Drew and I have, you have a lot of conversations about which Pop-Tarts are the best (strawberry with frosting) and which are just gross (pumpkin, which has no business being anything but jack-o'-lanterns or pie).

"Hey, do you know what to do if you ever get buried in an avalanche?" Drew says through a mouth full of Pop-Tart.

"Nope," I say. Drew's nana gave him *The Worst-Case Scenario Handbook* a couple of years ago, and he's read it cover to cover, fifteen times. Sharing techniques for surviving unlikely catastrophes is his favorite thing in the world besides fishing. "What should I do?"

"Spit in the snow," Drew says, and spits on the snowy yard.

"How's that going to help?"

"You make a little air pocket and spit, and then gravity will tell you which way is up and which way is down. Then you aim up and dig like crazy."

"Good to know." I wonder if I'm in for a whole day of survival training. "Hey, is Rachael coming fishing with us?" Drew's older sister is a senior in high school and the coolest person I know other than Abby. Rachael's the one who got me into Irish dancing, only she's way better at it. She was seventeenth in North America last year.

"Nah," Drew says through a bite of Pop-Tart. "She's got some dumb *feece* to go to."

"It's *feis*." I pronounce it the right way—*fesh*—even though Drew already knows that's what the Irish dance competitions are called. The plural is *feiseanna* (fesh-ee-AH-nuh). Drew always calls them *feces* instead. It drives Rachael nuts. "Where is this one?"

"Rochester, I think."

Part of me wishes I could be there to watch, but then I remember that ice fishing is going to help me pay for the solo dress for my own feis in Montreal later this month.

"Got decent tread on those boots?" Mrs. McNeill asks me, and I hold up a foot to show her.

"Nope," she says, and hands me a pair of ice cleats. "Wrap these around the bottom of your boots or you'll be slipping all over the place."

I do that while she and Drew load poles, augers, and bait buckets onto the sled. Then we head out onto the lake. Right by shore, there's a hole in the ice with a pile of shavings around it. "Were you out already?" I ask.

Mrs. McNeill nods and kicks at the circle of snow. "Drilled a hole to check the thickness. We have a good six inches, so we're all set." She leads us away from shore onto the clearest black ice.

The ice flowers are still here, but they're flat and muffled today, like wildflowers someone pressed in a book. They crunch under my feet as we head toward a point of land sticking out from shore.

I'm taking careful steps, one foot in front of the other, and managing to convince myself this is safe. But when we're halfway out to the point, the ice lets out a booming-loud, timpani-drum thump. I've heard muted ice sounds from shore before, but this is *loud*. I jump about a mile and look at Mrs. McNeill. "Is it breaking up?"

"I know how to survive being stranded on an iceberg," Drew says.

"I'm *so* hoping we don't need that information right now," I tell him.

Mrs. McNeill gives me a reassuring smile and shakes her head. "The ice is fine, my dear. You're simply hearing air bubbles working themselves up through the fissures now that the sun's up. Listen . . ." She pauses, and the ice booms again, like thunder out by the island a mile off shore. Then it makes a weird, video-game sound. *Gurgle-twang-zzzing!* "That's the ice talking, letting us know it's settling in for a good, long winter of fishing."

I keep going. But my heart's still pumping fast, and my legs feel wobbly, even with the cleats. If this ice really means to be reassuring, it ought to talk in something other than loud, scary growls and space invader weapon sounds. Right now, I'm hearing less "We're going to have a good winter" and more "I'm going to swallow you whole."

Not far from the point, Mrs. McNeill pulls the sled to a stop and looks around. "You think this is about where we were in the boat?" she asks Drew.

"Pretty close." Drew turns to me. "There's a ledge around here where the perch like to feed. We were pulling 'em in like crazy back in August."

They start unloading gear from the sled. I pick up an insulated bucket and can feel the bait sloshing around inside. "Are these minnows?"

"Yep. They're always better than lures when you can get 'em." Mrs. McNeill pulls a power auger from the sled and turns to Drew. "Shall we let Charlie give this a try?"

"Sure, as long as I get to drill my own," he says.

"I don't know how to use that," I say. The auger has a pull cord like the outboard motor on the McNeills' boat, and I couldn't pull hard enough to get that started last summer.

But Mrs. McNeill leans over to show me. "Piece of cake," she says. "Pull the rip cord." I do that, and the motor starts humming. "Great!" She points to a trigger thing on the auger's handle. "Now give it some gas to make the blades turn, and we're in business." She guides the auger to a spot on the ice and holds it with me, pressing down while the blades whirl into the ice. In a few seconds, there's a hole about six inches wide and a sparkling circle of ice shavings all around it. "Perfect!"

She hands the auger to Drew, who makes his own hole about ten feet farther out. Then he pulls three short fishing poles from the sled and hands one to me. It's only a couple feet long, way smaller than the poles we use in summer.

I take off my mittens, fish out a minnow, and bait the hook. My bare hands burn with the cold. Once they're mittened up again, Mrs. McNeill gives me a quick ice fishing lesson.

"You want to drop your bait maybe two or three feet down," she says, "and be sure to give the pole a good tug when you feel a bite. They can get away quick." She puts the lid on the bait bucket and slides it over so I can use it as a stool. "One more thing before you fish . . ." She reaches under her scarf, pulls out a four-leaf clover charm on a chain, and holds it up. "May the luck of the ice spirits be with you."

"That doesn't sound like science," I say.

She smiles and tucks the charm back under her layers of wool. "Drew's grandfather gave it to me when we got engaged years and years ago. He said it was a good luck charm, and I decided I'd believe that. It hasn't always worked for me, but I've learned that you take your magic where you can get it. Especially when you're waiting on fish to bite." She heads farther out on the ice, a little past Drew, to drill another hole, and I drop my line down under the ice to wait.

There's a lot of waiting in ice fishing, and now that I'm not moving, it feels a lot colder, even with the sunshine. The air is still biting, and my fingers never warmed up inside my mittens. I hold my pole with one hand and lift the other to my mouth to blow some heat onto them. Twenty minutes go by in silence, except for the ice groaning and thumping.

Finally, Mrs. McNeill stands up. "Got one!" she hollers, and reels in a perch.

Drew stands up to see. "Ain't big enough to bother with in the derby, but Billy'll take it."

"*Isn't*," Mrs. McNeill says. Drew totally knows better, but he loves the cowboys in old Western movies and knows it drives his nana crazy when he talks like them.

Mrs. McNeill pops the lid off her bucket, drops the fish inside, covers it, and sits down. Almost right away, she has another fish, and then Drew stands up. "I got one too!"

I keep waiting for a tug on my line. Drew pulls in three more fish, and Mrs. McNeill catches a bigger one. "This fella's got a chance, don't you think?" She holds it up, and Drew nods. She puts it in the bucket and calls to me. "Charlie, I bet you're in too shallow. Why don't you come out where it's a little deeper, and we'll set you up with a new hole?"

I shake my head. "I like this hole." That's because I'm pretty sure the water underneath it isn't over my head.

Another half hour goes by. Drew and Mrs. McNeill have at least twenty fish between them. I haven't even had a bite yet, but the thought of going out any farther on this ice makes my knees wobble. My hands are freezing, and my nose is running, and I can't remember why this seemed like a good idea. There's not much use fishing when you're afraid to go where the fish are.

Apparently, ice flowers don't have enough magic to turn me into a fisherman.

Fisherwoman.

Whatever. It's not going to happen.

"Woo-hoo!" Drew starts reeling in another one, and I'm about to give up when I feel the tiniest pull.

"Oh!" I stand up and give a tug, and at first I think the fish got away because it feels like I'm reeling in a whole lot of nothing. But when the line comes up, there's a tiny perch flopping on the end. It's not much bigger than the minnow I used as bait, but at least it's something.

"She's got one!" Mrs. McNeill shouts from across the ice.

Drew turns and looks. "You call that a fish?" He snorts out a laugh.

I ease my miniscule catch off the hook. "Should I let it go?"

"Nah, Billy'll take it. Put it in the . . . whoa!" Drew's pole almost jumps out of his hand. He turns around and starts reeling again. Mrs. McNeill's got another bite too. I stand up, holding the fish in one hand, and pull the lid off the bucket with the other.

"Please," someone says.

And I freeze. Because it's not Mrs. McNeill and it's not Drew. And it's not the stupid growly ice talking this time either. This voice is quiet and low-pitched and raspy.

"Please," it says again.

I look at the fish in my hand. It's a skinny thing, only about five inches long, black and green striped with orange on its fins. But instead of plain, glassy-black eyes like the other perch I've seen, this fish has bright-green eyes that almost glow. Like emeralds. Crystals. And this fish is looking right at me.

"Release me," the raspy voice says, and I swear I see the fish's mouth moving a tiny bit, as if it's gasping for breath.

But it can't be. Fish breathe through gills. That was one of Mrs. McNeill's lakeside science lectures last summer. And the bigger issue here is not how a fish breathes but that this one is talking. To me.

I look up at Mrs. McNeill and Drew, rebaiting their hooks. "Did you guys hear that?"

"Hear what?" Mrs. McNeill tips her head. The ice lets out a gurgle. "Oh, honey," she says, "those sounds aren't going to hurt you. I wish you'd come out a bit. You'd have more luck."

"I got another one!" Drew shouts. "Come on . . . be the big one!" He starts reeling again.

I stare down at the fish in my hand.

"Release me," the raspy voice says again, "and I will grant you a wish."

Kate Messner is a former middle-school English teacher and the author of the E. B. White Read Aloud Award winner *The Brilliant Fall of Gianna Z.* and its e-book companion, *The Exact Location of Home*; *Sugar and Ice*; *Eye of the Storm*; *Wake Up Missing*; *All the Answers*; *The Seventh Wish*; *Capture the Flag*; *Hide and Seek*; the Marty McGuire chapter book series; the Ranger in Time chapter book series; and several picture books. She lives on Lake Champlain with her husband and two kids. When she's not reading or writing, she loves hiking, kayaking, biking, and watching thunderstorms over the lake.

www.katemessner.com

@KateMessner

From **sweet** friendships
to **high-stakes** adventure
to **unexpected** magic—
**there's a lot to love
from Kate Messner!**

www.bloomsbury.com
Twitter: BloomsburyKids
Facebook: KidsBloomsbury

Looking for a little more danger?

Don't miss this utopian adventure from Megan Frazer Blakemore, where five friends must find the courage to change the world as they know it.

www.meganfrazer.com